# CITY OF LIES

## A COLLECTION OF SHORT THRILLERS

## SAM CHASE

First Edition

Editing by Jessica McKenna
Cover by Sam Chase

BEACHES AND TRAILS
PUBLISHING

# HUNTED

## A SHORT THRILLER

# CHAPTER 1
# SHADOWS IN THE CITY

THERE ARE ONLY two ways to stay hidden in plain sight: cling to the shadows or blend into the crowd. Tory Wayne chose the latter.

Each day, more than 800,000 worker bees buzzed through the streets of San Francisco, their collective hum offering her the perfect cover. She played it safe, avoiding trains and taxis; with both the police and mafia on her tail, giving anyone too long to study her face was an unnecessary risk. Staying in motion was survival.

It had been two years to the day since Tory last felt the stillness of dawn on the shore—a life flipped upside down in 730 days.

By now, she knew San Francisco's rhythm as intimately as her own heartbeat, anticipating the patterns of its busiest corners. Commerce was her cloak, and tourist-heavy spots like the Marina District and Pier 39 became convenient places to slip away, especially when she sensed eyes on her.

Each Christmas grew lonelier, but Tory had learned to settle into solitude.

Two days ago, the Union Square Ice Rink opened, nudging her with memories of a former life. For a split second, she thought about renting skates.

*Keep moving, idiot*, she warned herself.

Further down the bay, a patch of abandoned concrete near Pier 80 had recently sprung to life. Men in fluorescent vests filled the empty space each weekend, waving minivans into neat rows. Fifty dollars bought a parking spot just a block from the holiday market.

*Pure madness—but perfect cover.*

As she waited for the market to close, Tory kept to the shadows, eyeing the throngs of shoppers she would use to blend in on her way to the docks, and then to the station. The volume of families and strollers, even in the rain, took her by surprise. San Franciscans never let anything dampen their shopping spirit. Lord, have mercy.

Tory tossed her cigarette and buried her hands in the pockets of her leather jacket, her head down as she slipped into the crowd.

At Pier 80, she scanned the shoreline and cargo ships for activity. A contact had tipped her off the docks could yield secrets worth her time.

The docks were alive with shadows, flickering under the dim glow of worn-out streetlights. The oily sheen on the water mirrored pinpricks of light from anchored ships, while the low hum of engines vibrated across the bay. A damp chill clung to Tory's skin as she watched workers in stained overalls load and unload crates with a silent efficiency. The air was thick with the scent of fish and rusted metal, grounding her in the grittier underbelly of the Bay—a place where deals were struck, lives discarded like crates dropped into the sea.

An hour later, armed with intel, Tory grinned as she headed toward the train station. Irony never failed her; her devout, Creole mother would've cursed her for any part she played in a criminal life. Genetics, however, had gifted her with a five-foot-two frame perfect for evasion. Her curly black hair and rich, chocolate skin offered a handy cloak in dark spaces.

She knew to stay cautious during the city's in-between hours. Between six and nine, the buzz of the working day lulled into a hum, and just before the nightlife stirred, the streets were quiet. It was the window in which Tory felt most exposed.

San Francisco's darker corners came alive at night. Neon signs flickered above gritty storefronts, casting bruised hues across the cracked pavement. The smell of stale beer, cheap cologne, and garbage wafted through the alleyways as fog drifted in from the bay, clinging to the buildings like a ghostly veil. Tory had learned that laughter in these streets often masked danger, and every footstep felt like a beat in the city's pulsing, gritty rhythm—a rhythm that drew in both criminals and victims alike.

Approaching the Pier 80 Diamond Railroad Crossing, Tory knew she'd have to lie low in the subway station until the streets stirred back to life.

She had millions of hiding spots in the city—and Tory Wayne must have found half of them by now.

Cursing as she hit her head against a metal beam, Tory winced and rubbed her temple. Sore muscles, scrapes, bruises—a catalog of minor injuries, each one a testament to survival.

A faint breeze crept through the vents, carrying the scent of sweat, spilled drinks, and rust. Tory pressed herself against the steel, the grime clinging to her skin. From above, slivers of streetlight bled through, casting striped shadows over the litter-strewn floors. Down here, in the forgotten tunnels, she felt like she was walking through San Francisco's veins—dirty, tangled, and pulsing with secrets. Every creak and distant footstep set her nerves on edge.

Though the subway vents weren't designed for foot traffic, Tory found them a useful—if uncomfortable—route to the docks at dusk. She wasn't the only one. The vents had a reputation for harboring the city's desperate, marked with the literal stench of escape.

Tory ducked into a corner, waiting for a lull in foot traffic. When it came, she leapt up, popped off a vent cover, and hauled herself inside, carefully replacing it behind her.

She watched as the station below grew quiet.

Today's discovery had been valuable, but waiting still scraped at her patience. She'd uncovered hints of a deal between two of the city's top mafia bosses. William Frederickson and someone unknown. Her job—maybe her life—depended on finding out who. She adjusted her binoculars and scanned the terminal below.

The last train screeched to a halt. A few passengers hurried by, eyes forward.

Then, a confident click of expensive loafers broke the silence. They stopped directly below her. A chill snaked up her spine.

A dark figure in a trench coat adjusted the brim of his fedora, his strong cologne cutting through the stench.

"You can come down now, Wayne. It's rude to keep a guest waiting."

*Antonio Alvarez. How fitting.*

The sight of him dragged her past into stark focus. She stifled her nerves and jumped, landing on her feet with a smirk.

"Antonio. You still reek like a rat drowned in Bulgari," she shot, her lips curling.

Antonio crinkled his nose. "I'll take that over the stench you're sporting these days."

Years ago, Tory had built a decorated police career, honed her instincts to sniff out lies. But Antonio's expression was unreadable; something was different, and it set her further on edge. Whatever he was up to, it had to be big.

"Follow me," he said, turning toward the stairs.

"I'm not going anywhere with you," she replied, voice sharp.

"Then live like a subway rat. Or do as I say." Antonio didn't even turn around. He added, "I'm always saving your ass, Danger. This mistrust breaks my heart."

Propelled by urgency, Tory followed, her mind racing. She'd have loved the chance to stab him in the back herself someday.

His tailored suit drew stares, his height adding to the spectacle. But Tory realized he was also a black hole for attention—anyone watching him barely noticed her.

"How did you find me?" she asked.

"My associate saw you earlier," he said, finally meeting her gaze. The memory of the past flickered between them. Tory's heart drummed as she processed his words. Antonio scoffed. "You don't know what you're dealing with, Wayne."

"Then enlighten me," she fired back.

Antonio exhaled. "Stay out of it for a week. There's more at play than you realize."

In front of a rundown motel, he stopped. "Here we are."

Tory surveyed the chipped cherubs over the doors, bullet-pocked windows, and the faint aura of a once-luxurious, now grimy opium den. Antonio continued, "A friend runs this place. Lay low. One week. Don't cause trouble, and I'll throw you a bone."

Antonio stepped closer, face-to-face, until her instincts screamed. "You don't have a choice."

From across the street, a man saluted Antonio with two fingers, a rifle glinting in his hands. "So, what do you say?"

Tory gritted her teeth. "I trust you," she managed, tasting bile.

"Glad you understand," he said. "If George doesn't blow your brains out, I'll see you in a week."

# CHAPTER 2
# THE BEGINNING OF
# THE END

TWO YEARS *earlier*

Tory awoke with the sunrise, squeezing in a workout before pulling on her standard jeans, a Waite-branded T-shirt, and her leather jacket. She slung her badge around her neck and clenched a bagel between her teeth, arms full of case files she'd brought home the night before.

She was running behind, but her partner, Hank Waite, strolled up just as she reached the precinct, ensuring she wouldn't be the last to the morning briefing.

"Late to your own party, Wayne?" he grinned.

Hank was the most laid-back cop she'd ever met—rarely fazed, quick with a joke, always taking in everything with a calm, penetrating gaze. His charm disarmed people; suspects relaxed, spilled details they'd never share with a typical officer.

Tory was his opposite: eager and restless, theories swirling in her mind until she could lock them into place with hard evidence. Together, they made an effective team.

"Shut up; it's just a morning meeting. We have them every day." Tory shot him a wry smile.

"Oh, come on! You were in the Chief's office for an hour yesterday, wrapping up that murder case. He must have given you the promotion for nailing that confession," Hank pressed.

"You're always jumping to conclusions. Maybe that's why your case numbers are the lowest in the department," Tory quipped.

"It's because I have a life, and I don't bring case files home on a Friday night. I take home beautiful women—and sometimes men." He winked, then added, "But seriously, I'm your partner. Don't I get to hear about your promotion first?"

Tory sighed. Hank was persuasive, and the meeting was in five minutes. It couldn't hurt to tell him.

"Fine," she said, exasperated.

"Proud of you," Hank said, giving her a quick hug. "You deserve it more than anyone."

"Let's go. We're already late for my party," Tory joked.

The Chief waited in the conference room. Once the team's updates wrapped up, he cleared his throat.

"Everyone, join me in congratulating Tory Wayne. That's Captain Tory Wayne to you now. She's one of the most dedicated officers I've seen, and I'm confident she'll go far," he announced.

Clapping filled the room, but Tory shifted under the attention, especially as some male colleagues shot her looks, implying the promotion came easily. She squared her shoulders and ignored it.

As the meeting ended, a call came in, igniting the station.

"Wayne, Waite—you're heading downtown," the Chief said, his face grim. "Something big. No details yet."

"They always get the good cases," someone grumbled as Tory passed.

"Yeah, Chief has his favorites," added another, followed by a snicker.

Tory gritted her teeth. Let them talk. Right now, she had a case to focus on, and maybe it'd be big enough to drown out all the usual garbage.

---

THE WINTER AIR was colder than usual, biting as they arrived on-site. One benefit of finding bodies on a frosty morning was that they smelled less. The downside was everything else.

The forensics team dragged the evidence out from the pond's edge. Lucky for them, the victim had been shot; gunshot wounds were easier to identify than a mud-smeared corpse.

They quickly ID'd the victim as Sam Collins. He lay facedown, half-buried on the Bay's banks, with a dark red stain blooming across his back. The devil's rose—a gunshot while fleeing. Never a good sign.

Men like Sam Collins often followed a tragic pattern: impoverished backgrounds, organized crime affiliations, a short-lived run, then death by gunfire. Sam had lived with his grandmother, who was bedridden.

Tory's visit to the woman's cramped apartment served two purposes: to break the news and dig for information.

"He was a sweet boy," the woman whispered, voice raw. "Just twenty years old. He was going to college until I got sick. No insurance, no money. Sam never told me what he did to pay the hospital bills, but I knew. I knew they would break him."

Tory stood silent. Years of delivering bad news, and she still hadn't found a way to soften it. She'd learned that her job wasn't comfort; families turned to each other for that. Her job was to find answers, justice—and usually, she did.

"She's alone now," Hank said on their drive back.

"At least her end is near," Tory replied quietly. "Worse to leave the kids behind."

A grim but honest truth. Sam's grandmother wouldn't have to live long without him.

"Let's see what Bailey has to say." Hank pulled up to the precinct.

Dr. Bailey, their lead forensic analyst, greeted them with barely contained excitement.

"The gang messed up," he said, eyes gleaming. "They used a registered gun."

Bailey continued, "I analyzed the bullet wound—the gun is registered to Davos Sinclair himself."

No way.

Davos Sinclair, notorious arms dealer, ran a gun-smuggling empire feeding terrorist organizations along the East Coast, with rumored plans to expand internationally. And somehow, he'd slipped up.

"The Chief's bringing Davos in," Bailey added. "We caught him on multiple surveillance cameras near the scene with his son. There's even a record of Davos bailing Sam out when he was caught with coke a few months ago. Defense Attorney says we have a rock-solid case. We've got him."

Hank exhaled, a slow, satisfied whistle. "Well, I'll be damned."

"There's no way it's that easy," Tory muttered. "What's the catch?"

"Be optimistic, Wayne. Maybe we caught Davos red-handed."

---

IN INTERROGATION, Davos refused the coffee, careful not to leave DNA evidence. His lawyer, Carla Bronte, sat beside him, looking cool and confident. Carla had defended everyone from corrupt CEOs to serial killers, steel cloaked in polite smiles. If Tory had any respect for Carla, it was solely for her unflinching nerve.

"Good evening, detectives. Always a pleasure," Carla said, her tone saccharine.

"The pleasure's all ours, Miss Bronte," Hank replied smoothly.

"Let's cut to it," Tory said, her voice dry. "We've got your client cornered, Carla. This isn't a social call."

Davos exchanged a glance with Carla, who pulled a thick file from her bag.

"My client wants a plea deal," she announced.

Tory hadn't expected him to fold so quickly.

"He's looking at life in maximum security," Carla continued. "We'd like house arrest and a fifteen-year sentence instead."

"Not a chance," Hank scoffed. "He'll just run his empire from home."

Carla barely blinked. "You'll let this happen, Detective Waite, because my client's ready to name one of his associates."

Tory's pulse quickened. They didn't even have Davos booked on the weapons charges yet. Could he really be giving up someone significant?

"Do we have a deal?" Carla asked, arching an eyebrow. "Check with your chief if you must."

Fuming, Tory and Hank stepped out to confer with the Chief, who'd been watching from behind the glass.

"What do you think?" Tory asked.

The Chief's expression was unreadable. "Davos is fifty. Give him twenty years of house arrest, limited visitors. It's all we'll offer."

Back in the room, Tory delivered the counteroffer. "This is it. Or enjoy the next two decades peddling ramen behind bars."

Carla barely blinked. "My client accepts."

Hank clicked on the recorder. Tory folded her arms, watching Davos closely.

Davos leaned forward. "I've done business with William Frederickson in the past—legally, of course," he sneered.

Carla gave a small cough, a warning to keep it brief.

"But lately," Davos continued, "Frederickson's been making inquiries about rare metals. Deep-earth metals that are government-owned. Big things coming in, or so I hear."

"Maybe he's building a science lab for his kid," Tory drawled. "Still doesn't justify house arrest."

"I'm telling you, whatever he's got planned will put us all at risk," Davos replied, smirk gone. "The streets are being cleaned up for some massive operation."

The recorder clicked off, and Tory led Davos back to the guards. She studied him, looking for cracks in his composure.

"You gave up pretty easily," she probed.

Davos met her gaze. "Sometimes, you make sacrifices to win in the end."

"You didn't kill Sam, did you?" Tory ventured. "It was your son, and you took the fall."

Davos's silence confirmed it. Sam Collins was too insignificant for a man like Davos, but Davos Junior handled the recruits—showing them the ropes, breaking them in.

"You've got a job to do, Miss Wayne," he murmured. "Best of luck."

A FEW WEEKS LATER, Tory's luck had soured. To get closer to Frederickson, she'd taken a cover job as a maid in his estate—a sprawling fortress with a mansion that might as well have been a military base.

One of the senior maids, Jean, handed her a ridiculous, frilled uniform. "Mr. Frederickson believes in uniforms for staff."

Uniforms were just a way for Frederickson to categorize people instantly, Tory realized.

Tory spent her shift by the pool, passing towels to lounging men she assumed were low-level cronies. She looked around for familiar faces but saw none.

"Rose!" Jean's voice called sharply, for the third time.

Tory snapped to attention, mentally adjusting to her alias. "Yes, Jean?"

"Go dust the library, top to bottom."

Perfect. Alone in a library for hours.

Inside, Tory scanned the shelves, spotting a computer on a back desk. She moved quickly, downloading data, when footsteps sounded. Shit.

She pulled a cloth from her pocket, pretending to dust the keyboard.

A tall man stepped in, Bulgari cologne preceding him. Tory recognized the brand; favored by mobsters. But he was dressed as a groundskeeper.

"What are you up to?" he asked, eyes glinting with curiosity.

"Oh, just… checking my mid-term grades." She forced a smile.

He raised an eyebrow, smirking. "School, huh?"

"Community College. Accounting," she said. A safe story, if he asked.

"Well, I won't tell Jean," he winked. "I'm Antonio."

"Rose," she replied, exhaling relief.

She returned to her dusting as he walked away, but his parting words stuck with her:

"Or should I say, Danger?"

With a forced giggle, she turned away, waiting until his footsteps faded before tucking the USB into her bra.

# CHAPTER 3
# UNDERCOVER AT THE ESTATE

THE IRONCLAD EMPLOYMENT contract Tory signed surprised her, but the shocker was that Frederickson hired an outsider at all.

"No leaving the compound for the first two months—it's probation," Jean said. "You'll only use your devices in your quarters, and they'll be subject to random searches for unusual activity. Expect random pat-downs, too. No second chances in this place."

It was prison with a paycheck.

Tory had hidden an emergency beeper with a direct line to the precinct beneath the left wire of her bra, and now she'd tucked the USB stick under the right. Uncomfortable, but it kept her intel safe during pat-downs. The guards were all men, and they avoided that area.

She'd already coded Hank through the beeper to meet her at the estate's edge. She would hand him the USB tonight.

"Rose, come sit down. It's lunch," Jean called.

The grounds staff gathered at a long wooden table, the spread impressive—estate-grown fruits, vegetables, and a ridiculous amount of wine.

Turning to Jean, Tory leaned in. "You work long hours. Your grandkids must miss you a lot."

As Antonio had promised, Jean softened at the mention of her grandchildren.

"They do. Two grandsons, always getting into scrapes. My husband, Frank, will get a promotion soon, which means fewer hours here and more time with those boys."

Frank's up for a promotion, Tory noted. She listened patiently as Jean continued, watching the others grow looser over their drinks.

"Today, I dove for golf balls in the pool," Antonio scoffed.

"Lucky you. I made half a dozen trips from the pool to the boss's room for every little thing he 'forgot,'" another man joked.

"Enough complaining," Jean said sternly. "We're hosting an important meeting this weekend. Five guest rooms need to be spotless, and everyone must look their best. No slacking—I have eyes everywhere. Rose, I know you're new, but your dusting was abysmal."

Jean's tone softened. "First-day pass, but I expect everyone to double their efforts. These people are important."

Something big was coming.

---

THE NEXT DAY, Tory was assigned to the library again.

Lucky.

After pushing her cleaning supplies into a nearby closet, she hurried up the service staircase. There were cameras everywhere in the house, except on those stairs and within the main living quarters; Frederickson wouldn't want his private affairs caught on film.

Tory knew he had an office upstairs. Now she just had to find it. As she opened doors one after another, a prickle of tension ran through her with each turn of the knob.

Finally, she cracked open the right one. She paused at the threshold, eyeing the empty room.

*Alright, Wayne. Now what?*

Tory scanned for anything useful but knew that all the critical files were encrypted and stored digitally. She found a locked safe behind a tapestry, but couldn't crack it without her tools. She'd have to rely on surveillance.

Frederickson was due back in half an hour. Tory hinged her plan on his obliviousness to his own lavish surroundings. The large trunk in the corner looked decorative, so she climbed in, folding her uniform inside to shut the lid.

Tory, rarely religious, muttered a silent prayer.

Footsteps. "Antonio, get the boys."

It was Frederickson. *Here we go.*

She heard him shuffle papers, pour himself a drink, and then the sound of several pairs of boots entering the room.

"How was the trip to the city, boss?"

Tory recognized the voice—Rogers.

"Great, everything's coming up roses."

Frederickson's tone was smug. Tory listened intently, catching a mention of "Junior." The discussion painted a telling picture: Junior, unlike his father, wanted power now, fast and reckless. A voice snickered, "Kid wants to make his old man look like a saint." Their laughter held a tense edge, even Frederickson's, as if he feared what his son had become.

Another voice joined the mix—one with a faint lisp.

Frank. Tory recognized it immediately. So Jean's husband was indeed rising in the ranks.

"Was talking to the boss," Rogers snapped.

"He doesn't want small talk," another replied, annoyed.

A jangle of chains and heavy jewelry announced Costanzo's arrival.

"The docks are cleared, boss. Friday, during the holiday parade, the delivery will arrive."

Frederickson's voice cut through. "This is critical. Each crate must be verified with a Geiger counter. Low-level readings, or you've got bricks."

Tory's pulse quickened. Radioactivity? Davos was telling the truth. Why would he betray his son's operation?

"We're bringing 1,000 pounds of uranium ore," Frederickson continued. "When Junior arrives, show respect. I know he's a spoiled brat, but we need his daddy's lab connections to process the ore and his overseas ties to broker the deal with the Chinese. They'll pay cash and ship out our inventory by tanker."

Tory's stomach clenched. One thousand pounds of uranium? Hiroshima's bomb was just 140. The fallout from this transaction could go far beyond San Francisco; it was an international threat. And she had three days to stop it.

"After this, no one will be able to stop us," Costanzo declared. "We'll outnumber the police and rival families two-to-one in weapons. This city will be ours."

"What's the plan for Junior afterward?" Rogers asked.

"Let me handle that, boy. Junior's itching to prove himself. All we need is a 'yes' from him for now. Treat him nice on Friday. Maybe even take him out for lobster after. Every man deserves a good last meal."

So that was it. They were using Junior as a pawn, and Davos likely had no clue his son's role came with a death sentence.

Frederickson cleared his throat, raising his glass. "The sins of the father are visited on the son."

Glasses clinked, and they drank.

*Salute.*

---

ONCE SHE WAS certain they'd left, Tory slowly lifted the trunk lid. Noon sunlight filtered in, reminding her she hadn't missed lunch. Slipping back down the hall, she headed for the service staircase.

A voice stopped her. "What are you doing here, Danger?"

Tory turned, keeping her tone light.

"Looking for someone to complain to. Jean had me dust a thousand books for nothing. My arms are killing me."

"This isn't a place for mistakes," Antonio warned, his expression wary. "You won't get a second chance."

"Relax. Jean sent me to check the toilet paper in the bathrooms. Not exactly high-stakes," she replied breezily.

"Jean wouldn't assign you to this wing on your second day."

"What can I say? We're practically best friends now. Thanks to your advice about her grandsons," Tory grinned, deflecting with a wink.

Antonio studied her face, finally smirking. "You learn fast, Danger."

Unsure how to respond, Tory pivoted. "Coming to lunch? I'm starving."

Together, they headed down to the kitchen. In her hurry to avoid suspicion, Tory forgot to ask what Antonio had been doing upstairs.

# CHAPTER 4
# THE BETRAYER'S GAME

TORY SLIPPED from her room once everyone had gone to sleep. She checked her wristwatch—1:27 a.m. Almost time to meet Hank.

She opened the door silently and stepped outside, the sprawling grounds stretching before her. She would have to cross the woods along the property's edge to reach him.

The guards were switching shifts. With luck, she'd get out undetected, but timing was tight. Any misstep, any wandering guard, and she'd be a prisoner twice over.

The woods were dense and dark, offering Frederickson's men plenty of cover to position themselves if needed. Tory couldn't help but notice the wild beauty around her. Owls called from above, and possums scuffled through leaves. On any other night, she might have enjoyed the midnight solitude, but tonight her every nerve was on edge.

The farther she went, the thicker the shadows. Relax, Wayne, she reminded herself, though paranoia seeped in with each sound—rustling leaves, her own hurried breathing, the night's alive whispering. Navigating the maze of branches and underbrush, she reassured herself that no one could tail her, not out here.

As insects crept over her skin, Tory's mind flashed to cases where bodies, days dead, lay half-buried under layers of grime. This is nothing. But a pang of claustrophobia gnawed at her, as if the forest itself closed in.

Ahead, a sliver of moonlight cut through two trees. She pushed forward and nearly stumbled.

Inching along the electric perimeter fence, she scanned the darkness for Hank.

"Hey, Wayne. You made it."

Hank's voice hit her like a lifeline.

"I'm not sure how you got here. This place is a fortress," Tory muttered, eyes still scanning.

"I could say the same. Smells like you went overboard on the cologne," Hank joked, coughing faintly.

They froze. Even a small sound could betray them.

She rolled her eyes, whispering, "Glad I risked my neck just to get roasted." She passed the USB through a gap in the electrified wire. "I hacked the library computer and downloaded the data here. Sync it to a precinct server ASAP."

Hank pocketed it. "What did you find?"

"Frederickson's plotting a nuclear deal—Friday night, at the docks. He's using Davos Junior to run the operation, then plans to kill him afterward. Everyone who matters will be there to see the deal through, and they're bringing the suppliers back here. It's our best chance to take them all down in one sweep."

Hank's face was shadowed, but she could see his eyes widen. "Holy shit, Wayne. I'll take care of it. Good work."

Just as she was about to turn back, static crackled from a guard's walkie-talkie. She stiffened as footsteps crunched closer.

Tory froze, heart pounding. She scanned the grounds for cover—a lone gazebo lay ahead. She'd have to run for it.

But a firm hand clamped her elbow from behind. She spun, fists ready to swing, when a familiar voice hissed, "What the hell, Danger? I told you not to pull this shit."

Antonio. Perfect timing.

"What's your excuse this time?" he demanded. "Actually, don't bother. Tell me the truth, or I'm taking you straight to Frederickson."

Tory's options were razor thin. Antonio wasn't a gang member; he was just on Frederickson's payroll. Maybe he'd respect the badge over loyalty to a billionaire criminal. She took a leap.

"I'm a cop," she whispered.

Antonio's expression barely shifted. He simply nodded, which surprised her more than anything.

The tension between them hung heavy until a flashlight beam arced through the darkness.

"Both of you, stop," the guard ordered, gun aimed.

"Put that away, Hector," Antonio snapped, sounding irritated. "You're ruining the mood."

Antonio pulled Tory closer, as if sharing a secret, and Hector scowled but lowered the gun.

"No one's supposed to be out after lights out," Hector warned.

"We just wanted some time alone," Antonio replied, laughing.

Tory's face flushed, and she forced herself to look down, letting Hector read into the situation.

"Fine. Back to your rooms now," Hector grumbled, stalking off.

Thank God. Or whatever.

---

SUNLIGHT SLASHED through Tory's sleep like a blade. She sat up, every inch of her body aching. The scratches on her arms and legs convinced her she hadn't imagined the midnight trek. After dressing, she met the others in the breakfast room.

Antonio had saved her a seat next to him. He leaned close as she sat, voice low. "We need to talk after breakfast."

Tory nodded, and they ate in silence.

At 9 a.m. sharp, Jean shooed everyone to their posts. Tory gathered her plate, heading for the kitchen, with Antonio following.

They finally stopped by the sink, where he bent down to whisper in her ear, "I'm undercover too."

A cold shock traveled down her spine. She froze, but before she could respond, he was already leaving.

She closed her mouth just as Jean entered.

"No dawdling, Rose! To the library, now!"

Finally, she thought. The library was the one place no one ever intruded, and today, dusting the shelves offered a rhythm that allowed her to plan. She pictured the raid—reinforcements, snipers stationed in nearby buildings, plainclothes cops posing as street vendors.

Her thoughts were interrupted by footsteps.

"I'm surprised to find you working, Danger," Antonio smirked.

He studied her, the look on his face unreadable.

"We should talk," he said, dropping the usual banter.

She kept her tone neutral. "We got a tip on Frederickson. Chief, put me on the case."

He nodded, his voice shifting. "I work for Junior—Davos's son. Junior's taking over."

Tory's pulse quickened. The tension between them was almost palpable, as if Antonio had drawn a line she couldn't yet see.

"You do understand that implicates you?" Tory asked, raising an eyebrow.

"I do," Antonio replied, his voice steady. "And I know you won't turn me in."

She folded her arms. "You're awfully sure of yourself."

"We've both got skin in the game, Rose—or whatever your real name is."

Antonio's raised brow silently invited her to fill in the blank. She didn't oblige.

"You're going to have to trust me," he continued. "Starting now."

There was a tightness in his voice, as if it cost him something to say it. He turned away; the mask slipping back over his face, leaving her wondering if she'd ever get a glimpse of what lay beneath.

"What makes you so confident?" she pressed.

"Because Frederickson wants to see you. Right now. And you're going to come with me."

Tory's eyes widened. Is this already a disaster?

"It'll be fine," Antonio reassured her, though his eyes betrayed a flicker of tension.

With no other choice, she followed him down the hall.

SHE ATTEMPTED to tramp up the staircase, hoping it might suggest she could never sneak anywhere, let alone into Frederickson's office. She also took Antonio's hand—overkill, maybe — but it softened the moment. His demeanor was fluid, adaptable, which only made him harder to read.

In front of Frederickson's study, Tory took a deep breath.

"Boss."

Frederickson glanced up, acknowledging Antonio before his gaze fixed on Tory. "Rose, is it?"

She nodded.

Frederickson lounged behind his desk, sleeves rolled to reveal tattooed arms, and shut his laptop.

"Thank you, Antonio. You can wait outside."

Antonio slipped away, leaving her alone.

"Sit, Rose." Frederickson's stare was unblinking. He was younger than she'd expected, his dark eyes intense and calculating.

"So, how do you like working here?" he asked, almost conversationally.

"It's… it's a good place, Mr. Frederickson."

"Call me Fred. Only my father called me William, and he's dead," he said, flashing a smile that didn't reach his eyes.

"Yes, Fred," she stammered.

"Great. You seem to follow rules well—except last night," he continued, leaning back.

"I'm sorry—"

"Sorry doesn't cut it. We run a tight ship. Pretty young women tend to have… certain desires. You could do better than sneak around with one of my men."

Frederickson rose, circling her with unsettling ease. He slipped a hand to the small of her back, too close, his eyes searching her face.

"I understand—"

"Do you, Rose? Because everything here belongs to me. It'd be a shame if a pretty thing like you had an accident."

His fingers brushed her cheek, twisting a strand of her hair. His gaze was piercing, his proximity suffocating.

"Yes, I understand," she said, meeting his gaze with all the steadiness she could muster.

"Good," he replied, his voice dripping with satisfaction. "I trust there won't be any more... misunderstandings."

Frederickson opened a drawer and retrieved a garish bracelet, motioning for her wrist. She gritted her teeth as he fastened it on, his smile full of dark satisfaction. It was a mark, a claim. Whatever Antonio had told him had kept her alive, but this wasn't dignity.

An abrupt knock sounded at the door.

"What is it?" Frederickson snapped.

Jean's voice filtered through. "I have something important, sir."

Frederickson waved Tory off, and she bolted past Jean. In the library, she slumped against the wall, body still humming with adrenaline.

This is all falling apart.

In another wing of the house, Antonio splashed water on his face, staring at his reflection.

"She's going to ruin everything," he whispered. "I'll have to make her disappear... without making her disappear."

---

Jean burst into Tory's quarters at 7 a.m., annoyingly chipper.

"Why aren't you up, Rose? Today's your day off, but you have to attend Frederickson's address in 30 minutes. No one's allowed out afterward, understand?"

Tory nodded, relieved she had the day to herself. She joined the others downstairs, noting the large podium set at one end of the room.

Frederickson stepped up, voice confident. "Some of you haven't met me, but I know all of you. I appreciate your dedication."

Tory exchanged a glance with Antonio, who muttered, "Is he talking to the mayor or us?"

Frederickson continued, "We're expanding, and it'll be a microscope for some of you. Others won't fit our future, but remember, you'll always be a part of the Frederickson family. 'Til death do us part.'"

Tory's stomach clenched as Frederickson cast a knowing glance her way. She'd forgotten the bracelet.

Thinking fast, she turned sharply, pulling Antonio into a close embrace, tucking her wrist out of sight.

"Meet me in the cellar bar at five," he murmured, hiding the urgency with a casual smile.

Tory returned to her room, forcing herself to wait. When the time came, she dressed and slipped out, mind racing.

---

MUSIC AND LAUGHTER spilled from the cellar bar. Tory listened at the door.

"I told you she'd come, boss. I'm a man of my word," Antonio said, his voice carrying inside.

Peeking in, Tory saw Antonio and Frederickson waiting. Her heart dropped—she wasn't wearing the bracelet. She rushed back to her room, secured it, and returned to the bar, hoping her nerves wouldn't betray her.

"Rose, nice of you to join us," Antonio greeted smoothly, motioning to a glass set at her place. Her skin crawled as she sat beside Frederickson.

"This cocktail's my twist on the Old Fashioned. I call it 'The Mole,'" he said with a glint in his eye.

The name didn't escape her notice. Keeping her hand steady, she swirled the drink, showing off the bracelet.

Tory drank, her mouth puckering from the smoky bourbon.

As the drink went down, so did her memory.

The morning alarm felt deafening. She stumbled to the bathroom, nausea flooding over her. Flashes of last night returned. Frederickson's laugh, his hands too close. Antonio's cologne lingered on her skin.

Back in her room, Tory realized with dawning horror: her beeper was gone. She frantically searched but found nothing.

Downstairs, she stormed into breakfast.

"Finally joined us, I see," Antonio smirked, sounding more like Frederickson than himself.

She tried to control her voice. "What happened last night?"

Antonio's mouth quirked in amusement. "Relax, Danger. You can't hold your liquor. I just got you to bed. All above board. Scout's honor."

Am I supposed to believe that?

# CHAPTER 5
# LINES DRAWN IN BLOOD

HANK WAS busy charting Friday's bust plan, his notepad a mess of scribbled departments, positions, and timings, like a chaotic football playbook. Tory's "Type A" touch was sorely missed.

The Chief's voice cut through his thoughts. "Waite, you've got a visitor."

*Odd. I wasn't expecting anyone.*

Hank followed the Chief to the interrogation room. Inside, a man dressed in a Waite polo and tan pants looked like he'd strolled off a department store ad—and straight out of one of the city's largest criminal organizations.

As Hank took the seat opposite his guest, a heavy waft of familiar cologne hit him, noxious and unmistakable.

*Where have I smelled that before?*

Hank opened the file waiting on the table and read aloud, "Antonio Alvarez, police informant, currently employed by the Frederickson crime family of San Francisco."

Antonio shifted in his chair, visibly irritated at "police informant."

"And it says here you specifically requested me," Hank continued, his tone steady. "Mind telling me why you tied me to Frederickson? There are more senior officers here. Consider this question a test."

Smooth as butter, Antonio replied, "You and your undercover detective weren't alone in the woods the other night."

---

TORY SPRANG from bed Friday morning before her alarm. She ran to the window, heart pounding.

*A squad car. Hank must be here.*

She donned her maid's uniform and headed to breakfast, trying to keep her expression neutral. She couldn't risk tipping anyone off.

Hank was in the dining hall, talking with Jean. But as soon as Tory walked in, he straightened and turned toward her.

"Rose Winegard, I'm taking you to the station. You're under arrest."

Hank placed a firm hand on Tory's shoulder, spinning her around as he clicked the handcuffs onto her wrists. She didn't have to fake surprise; confusion rolled through her mind.

*What's your play here, Hank?*

The cool metal of the cuffs dug into her wrists as Hank led her toward his squad car, her mind racing with questions and doubts.

Settling in the backseat, Tory caught Hank's quick glance through the rearview mirror. She gave a forced laugh. "Taking this a bit far, aren't we, partner?"

"Tory Wayne, you are under arrest. You have the right to remain silent. Anything you say can and will be used against you in a court of law. You have the right to an attorney."

Her amusement faded. *He's serious.*

Rain splattered across the car windows as they sped away from the estate in silence. When they reached the station, Hank split off, leaving her to go through the familiar intake process with the other officers. Eyes followed her as she was paraded through the station in cuffs; whispers and gawking filled the corridor. When they reached the end, a guard led her into a small room, where she changed into state-issued clothes, feeling exposed in a way she hadn't since going undercover.

They brought her, cuffed, to the interrogation room.

The irony wasn't lost on her. This was her first time on this side of the table.

Hank entered and tossed a thick envelope across the table, spilling a spread of photographs.

"Explain," he said flatly, his eyes cold.

Tory glanced down at the photos: Frederickson in a jewelry shop, a bracelet box open in his hand, and him clasping the bracelet onto her wrist. Another showed Frederickson's hand on her thigh in the cellar bar, her head tilted back, laughing. A wave of memories crashed over her.

"Someone tipped Frederickson off. We had to call off the bust." Hank's voice sliced through her thoughts. "We've got an inside informant—"

His words faded as her mind flashed back to that night in the bar: Frederickson pouring her drink, Antonio slipping out, the expensive bourbon, Frederickson's laugh, his hand on her thigh. The haze in her mind lifted, and she realized who the informant was.

*Antonio.*

---

THE GUARDS SHOULD HAVE KNOWN BETTER than to leave Tory Wayne alone in a holding cell overnight. She knew every flaw in this place: loose pins in the cell door and a ten-minute gap during the midnight shift change.

She lifted the cell door slightly, feeling for the pins, carefully nudging each into alignment. Freedom.

Moving quickly, she ducked into the janitorial closet. Stripping down, she yanked a large black trash bag over herself, poking holes for her head and arms, then stuffed her uniform with toilet paper and positioned it under her blanket on the cot. It wouldn't pass for long, but a few extra minutes might be all she needed.

Footsteps.

She froze as a guard lumbered in, then settled into the desk chair with a magazine. After a long, silent pause, he got up and walked out.

*Now or never.*

Tory slipped out, carefully closing the cell door behind her. She padded down the hall, heart pounding as she reached the exterior door just as the alarm blared.

***

WEARING HER GARBAGE-BAG DISGUISE, Tory arrived at Frederickson's estate. The electric fence loomed in front of her.

*Think, Wayne.*

She spotted a branch stretching just beyond the fence. A rusted pipe lay half-buried in the ground nearby. If she could get the leverage to reach the limb, she could climb over.

She wedged the pipe into the dirt, took a running start, and launched herself upward. As her body rose, a gust of wind blew the garbage bag over her face. Not now.

Her fingertips grazed the branch. She hooked her hand around it and swung her legs up, clinging to the bark.

Morning workouts finally paid off.

***

ONCE INSIDE THE ESTATE GROUNDS, Tory moved through the thick woods, bleeding and sore. A twig snapped behind her. She stilled, hearing two muffled voices—Frederickson and another man.

A hand clamped over her mouth. She spun, ready to fight, but froze at the familiar scent.

"Shh," Antonio whispered, then pointed his finger to his ear.

Frederickson's voice drifted through the trees. "Send word to the Made Men. I want Tory Wayne—dead or alive. There's a bounty on her head."

Antonio released her as the voices faded.

"What are you doing here, Rose?" he asked, his smirk faintly mocking.

"Cut the bullshit, Antonio. You know I'm not Rose."

He studied her for a moment, his eyes trailing over her makeshift outfit.

"What I don't know," he replied coolly, "is why you're here. You were safe in jail."

Safe. Antonio's words twisted like a knife, and she realized the depth of his betrayal. She took a deep breath, jaw clenched.

"You turned on me."

Antonio shrugged. "It was never personal, Danger. I knew you were a cop as soon as I followed you into the woods. Junior's invested in this deal, and I'm here to protect his interests. I couldn't blow my cover—so I blew yours."

Her anger flared, and she stepped close. "And where's my beeper? Did you touch me that night in the cellar with Frederickson?"

Antonio's gaze didn't waver. "I have no idea what you're talking about. I didn't rat you out to Frederickson—only to Hank. I needed him to get you out clean and to spook Frederickson enough to cancel the deal."

He's telling the truth, she realized, though the thought barely soothed her fury. She'd been played by her own team and the enemy.

"So what now?" she demanded.

Antonio met her glare evenly. "You stay out of sight. Frederickson's gunning for you, and I can't help you if you get caught again. Leave while you can."

Tory's mind spun, her thoughts blazing with unanswered questions. Antonio's motives were his own. But if she wanted to take down Frederickson, she'd have to trust someone—even if it meant trusting the man who'd just double-crossed her.

As she watched him slip back into the shadows, one thing became clear: the only way out was to clear her own name and prove her innocence.

# CHAPTER 6
# THE RAID

PRESENT-DAY

Each morning, Tory awoke in the same dingy apartment, her mind rejecting the reality until she opened her eyes. Antonio had hidden her here after their escape through the subway vents. Across the alley, George remained ever watchful, endlessly polishing his sniper rifle.

Today was no different. The apartment was a box, every corner visible from where she stood.

But today, something broke the monotony. An envelope lay on the floor near the door. Tory rose slowly, stretching her arms to the ceiling before casually sweeping her hand down to pick up the envelope and tucking it into her waistband. She moved to the bathroom, the only place with privacy.

Inside, she tore it open, pulling out a note, a small key, a wad of $100 bills, and her old undercover beeper. The note read:

*"It was all business, Danger. Never personal."*

Antonio. But did George know about this? Tory glanced out, seeing George at his post. She turned her attention back to the key, a small, silver one, and stepped back into the main room. It fit the deadbolt.

Free for the first time in days, Tory wasted no time. She needed prints from the beeper and made her way across the city to Dr. Bailey's lab.

---

BAILEY DIDN'T RUN the prints herself but led Tory to a contact in Chinatown—a discreet forensics expert, Dr. LeeAnn Shultz, who handled cases for both defense attorneys and, occasionally, the mob. Shultz wasn't above tweaking her results for a bribe. Tory approached a plain pine door with iron hardware and slipped inside without knocking.

The entryway was empty, save for an unoccupied reception desk. Ignoring the bell, Tory moved down the hall, opening the first door she found to a stark, no-nonsense lab. A woman in a white coat spun around.

"Tory Wayne, I presume," she said with a brisk nod. "Bailey called. I'm Dr. Shultz."

"I need prints from this beeper," Tory said, handing it over.

Shultz took it with a gloved hand. "I'll have something in an hour."

Tory hesitated, then pulled out a small bag holding a single hair clipping. "One more thing. Run a tox screen on this hair sample. It's mine."

Shultz took the bag and nodded, and Tory left the lab to kill an hour.

---

WHEN TORY RETURNED, the reception desk was occupied by a college-aged guy spilling over the sides of his chair. Half-chewed Cheetos rolled in his mouth as he mumbled, "Name?"

"Wayne. Tory Wayne."

The kid handed her a sheet of paper, unevenly folded, its edge stained with Cheetos dust. Tory forced herself not to flinch as she grabbed it. After entering something on his keyboard, he looked up.

"That'll be $600."

She paid and left without a word, her stomach churning.

Back on the bustling streets of Chinatown, Tory read the results as she moved with the crowd. The hair sample tested positive for GHB—she had been drugged. It was no surprise, just confirmation. But the print report on the beeper was a shock: her own prints, Hank's, Antonio's—and Jean Stoddard's.

Jean's face flashed in Tory's mind. She remembered the twisted look on Jean's face the night Frederickson ordered her to bring bourbon. Jean had been there in the cellar bar the night Tory was drugged.

The results were dated December 6th. A week had yet to pass, which meant the dock deal was still set for the next day. She still had time.

Tory pocketed the report and made her way to Bailey's lab.

---

BAILEY WASN'T THRILLED to see her.

"Tory, I told you, that was all I could do. You're putting me in a bad spot," Bailey said.

"I just need you to deliver these to Hank," Tory pressed, placing the beeper and results sheet on the counter. "Say it was left in your mailbox anonymously. You don't have to explain anything. Bailey, I'm out of options. This is my life we're talking about."

Bailey's face softened. "Fine. But this is the last time, Tory. Good luck."

Relieved, Tory headed back to Pier 80. The streets buzzed with tourists, and she blended into the crowd. She spent the rest of the day camped out at the subway station opposite the pier, watching the light fade and staying still as a statue. Someone tossed a quarter at her feet, and she realized she must have looked like a bum.

As darkness fell, she climbed into the overhead vent system. The enclosed space reeked, but it was the safest place she knew.

---

THE SHARP RAT-A-TAT-TAT of a semi-automatic rifle jolted her awake.

*What the hell?*

Tory scrambled from the vent, darting up the stairs. She emerged just west of the docked cargo ship, where William Frederickson lay facedown in a spreading pool of blood. His lifeless body was marked by a dark, widening oval of crimson.

Her eyes snapped from Frederickson's corpse to the approaching SWAT team, led by Hank. She barely ducked out of sight as the officers seized Junior and Frederickson's top aides—Rogers, Costanzo, Frank...and Jean?

Shock hit her just as something struck her head from behind. Darkness flooded in, but as she slipped into unconsciousness, she heard a familiar voice.

"I told you to stay away, Danger."

---

WHEN TORY CAME TO, she was lying stuffed inside the vent again, her head throbbing. A touch to the back of her skull revealed no blood; only the cold, damp condensation made her hair wet.

It was dark outside. She didn't know how long she'd been out or if Antonio planned to return. But she knew the vent was no longer safe.

Carefully, she crept out. Police tape surrounded the docks, fluttering in the night wind. It must have been at least 24 hours since the bust. By now, Hank would have Bailey's delivery. With luck, he'd understand what had happened.

For the first time in two years, Tory walked openly down the center of an empty street, shoulders back. She'd either cleared her name or lost everything. She moved slowly, savoring what might be her last taste of freedom.

After ten blocks, Tory reached the station. The automatic doors opened, and Hank was waiting by the front desk.

As Hank's footsteps faded, Tory felt a heaviness settle over her. Alone on the damp street, she looked into the night, trying to remember the woman she'd been when she first wore a badge. Back then, the city had seemed smaller, her power clearer, as if she could change things. Now, with every step into Frederickson's world, right and wrong had blurred.

Here she was, relying on Antonio and hiding truths from her own force. Was this loyalty or something darker? Tory took a shaky breath, wondering if this mission would consume her before it ended.

# CHAPTER 7
# A DANGEROUS ALLIANCE

THE NIGHT AIR was heavy with smoke and distant sirens. Tory leaned against the cold concrete wall outside the station, letting the weight of the last few days settle over her. The raid had been a success —Frederickson and several of his top associates were in custody. She had guided Hank's team through the maze of Frederickson's estate, slipping between shadows, fighting off guards, and steering them to places only she had access to. But beneath the surface of victory, a chill lingered.

Inside, the police station buzzed with activity as detectives shared intel and forensics combed through the raid's evidence. Hank joined her outside, his face drawn but relieved.

"Good work in there," he said, leaning beside her. "We couldn't have done it without you."

She nodded, watching the city lights flicker. "But is it enough? Taking down Frederickson?"

Hank hesitated. "Frederickson was a big player, but he's not the only one. Junior and some of his top men got away. Word is they're regrouping, waiting for the dust to settle before making their next move. We disrupted things, but we didn't end them."

Tory's jaw tightened. She'd risked everything to infiltrate Frederickson's operation, putting herself through unimaginable danger. And yet, even with Frederickson gone, she could still feel the weight of his influence—and his men—circling like sharks.

Hank seemed to sense her unease. "Listen, there's something else. The higher-ups...they're questioning your methods. Some don't like how close you got, especially with Antonio involved."

Tory's gaze hardened. "So after everything I did, they're questioning my loyalty?"

Hank shook his head. "It's politics, Tory. They think you got too close, that maybe you'll look the other way if Antonio makes a move to fill Frederickson's place."

A flicker of anger surged beneath her fatigue. "So they'd rather lose the city than trust an undercover cop who actually got results."

"Just watch your back," Hank said. "Right now, the people upstairs aren't any more reliable than the ones we're fighting."

She looked away, unwilling to let him see the hurt beneath her anger. She'd given everything for this job, and still it was never enough. Even Hank's warning stung, a reminder that her loyalty would always be questioned, her actions suspect.

As she turned to leave, Hank reached into his pocket. "Oh, this came for you. Some guy left it at the front desk, in and out before anyone could ID him."

He handed her a slim, unmarked envelope. Inside, she found her missing SOS beeper, a stack of crisp hundred-dollar bills, and a small note in bold, slanted handwriting.

*"Remember, even shadows need the light to survive."*

Her pulse quickened—she didn't need a signature to know it was from Antonio. The man she still couldn't fully trust, yet couldn't entirely sever from her life.

She pocketed the envelope, keeping her face neutral. "You say some guy dropped this off?"

Hank shrugged. "No idea. Just a hooded figure. Like I said, in and out."

Tory felt the weight of the envelope against her side. Antonio's message was clear: he wasn't done with her yet. Whatever he had planned would require her involvement—or her complicity.

---

BACK IN HER TINY APARTMENT, Tory laid the envelope's contents on her kitchen table. She turned the beeper over in her hand, the memories of Frederickson's mansion rushing back. Antonio had been there in those final moments, helping her escape. But why? Was he really on her side, or was he just using her for his own advantage?

Her thoughts drifted to Junior, Frederickson's escaped lieutenant, whose ruthlessness rivaled his father's. If Antonio intended to rise within the criminal hierarchy, Junior would be his first obstacle—or perhaps his next ally. The thought left her uneasy, a sense of dread pressing down on her.

She leaned back, staring at the note until the words blurred. "Even shadows need the light to survive." Was Antonio offering her protection? A partnership? Or was this just another reminder of how deeply entangled she'd become in this web of lies?

---

TORY'S PHONE BUZZED, pulling her from her thoughts. The message was from an unknown number. She clicked it open, her eyes narrowing as she read:

*"Junior is planning a return. And this time, he won't make the same mistakes."*

Her grip tightened around the phone. Junior was more than a successor; he was a force, restrained for too long. His ambition was different, reckless and impatient. If he was coming back, it wouldn't just be for revenge—it would be to claim everything his father had built. He wouldn't stop until he had crushed anyone in his way.

With one last look at Antonio's note, Tory knew she couldn't back down. Whatever fractured alliances and dangerous moves lay ahead, she was ready. If Antonio thought he could manipulate her, he'd soon learn she wasn't anyone's pawn.

The End

# FRACTURED

## A SHORT THRILLER

# CHAPTER 1
# FRAMED

THE SHARP METALLIC tang of blood hung in the air, its bite sharper than the chill seeping through the cracked concrete walls. Tory Wayne stepped carefully into the warehouse, her boots crunching on shards of broken glass scattered across the floor. Overhead, a single fluorescent light flickered erratically, throwing harsh shadows across the chaos.

It had all the hallmarks of a syndicate hit—a body slumped against the far wall, blood pooling beneath it in a dark, viscous spread. But this one was different. Her name was stamped all over it, whether she wanted to believe it or not.

Vincent Herrera, a syndicate lieutenant, stared lifelessly at the ceiling, his glassy eyes catching the pale light. A single gunshot wound marred his chest, precise and deliberate. Not a warning shot—an execution.

Tory crouched beside the body, her leather jacket creaking faintly as she moved. Her fingers hovered near the envelope tucked neatly into Herrera's pocket. Everything about it screamed trap, but she couldn't walk away without answers.

The paper inside was damp with blood, its corners fraying. Her name, printed in bold black letters, hit her like a punch to the gut: *Tory*

*Wayne.* Below it, a short, taunting message sent ice crawling up her spine.

*Nice try, Tory.*

Her heart pounded as her thoughts raced. The envelope felt heavier in her hand than it had any right to be. This wasn't just a warning—it was a statement. Someone had gone to great lengths to make her look guilty.

The wail of sirens broke her trance, faint at first but growing louder with every passing second. Flashing blue and red lights reflected off the warehouse windows, each pulse of color pushing her closer to panic.

"Damn it," she muttered, shoving the envelope into her pocket and standing. She had minutes, maybe seconds, before the cops arrived. The fact that someone had tipped them off wasn't a coincidence—it was part of the setup.

Tory scanned the warehouse, her sharp green eyes landing on a side door partially hidden by stacks of crates. She moved quickly, her boots echoing faintly against the concrete as she slipped through the door into the brisk night air.

---

THE ALLEY OUTSIDE was a maze of rusted shipping containers and narrow pathways choked with shadows. The sirens were closer now, the sound bouncing off the walls around her. Tory pulled her phone from her pocket, her fingers shaking slightly as she dialed.

The line clicked after the first ring.

"Wayne, where the hell are you?" Detective Harrison's voice cut through the tension like a blade, sharp and accusing.

"Harrison, listen to me," Tory said, her voice low and urgent. "I've been set up. Someone wants me to take the fall for—"

"You think I don't know?" he interrupted, his tone harsh. "We've got a dead body at Pier 14, witnesses placing you at the scene, and evidence pointing straight to you. If you want to explain yourself, you'd better come in."

"Harrison, you know me—"

"What I know," Harrison said, his voice colder now, "is that I've got orders to bring you in. And if you don't come willingly, it's not going to end well."

The line went dead, leaving Tory gripping the phone in silence.

She leaned against a rusted container, the chill of the metal seeping through her jacket. Harrison had always been one of the good ones, but now even he was being pulled into this. Whoever had orchestrated this setup wasn't just framing her—they were dismantling any chance she had at defending herself.

The faint screech of tires snapped her out of her thoughts. A squad car pulled into the alley, its headlights sweeping the narrow passage. Tory ducked into the shadows, her hand instinctively moving to the pistol holstered beneath her jacket.

She didn't draw it. Shooting a cop, even in self-defense, would cement her guilt in ways she couldn't afford.

The officers stepped out of the car, their flashlights cutting through the darkness.

"Wayne, we know you're here!" one of them called, his voice firm but laced with tension.

Tory's pulse quickened. She slipped deeper into the alley, her steps careful and silent. The fire escape above her caught her eye, its rusted metal barely visible in the dim light. She moved quickly, grabbing the ladder and hauling herself up.

The steel groaned beneath her weight, the sound sharp against the quiet. She froze, listening for any sign that the officers had heard her. When their voices carried on below, she continued, climbing to the rooftop.

From her vantage point, Tory could see the officers searching the alley, their flashlights sweeping across the ground. Her breath came in shallow bursts as she crouched behind a ventilation unit, watching them move.

One of them paused, his flashlight lingering on the fire escape. Tory's heart pounded as he stepped closer, his gaze following the ladder's rusted rungs upward.

The crackle of a radio broke the tension.

"Suspect spotted near the docks," the dispatcher said.

The officers exchanged a glance before turning back to their car. Tory exhaled slowly as they drove off, the sirens fading into the distance.

She leaned back against the ventilation unit, her thoughts racing. Whoever was pulling the strings had planned this down to the second. They wanted her desperate, isolated, and with no one to turn to.

No one except Antonio Alvarez.

---

AN HOUR LATER, Tory found herself standing outside a dimly lit bar in the Mission District. The neon sign above the door flickered faintly, its red glow casting jagged shadows across the cracked pavement.

The smell of stale beer and cigarette smoke hit her as she stepped inside. The bar was quiet, the low murmur of conversation punctuated by the occasional clink of glasses.

Tory's sharp eyes scanned the room, landing on Antonio in the far corner. He leaned back in his seat, his dark eyes calm but watchful as he sipped his drink.

"Wayne," he said as she slid into the booth across from him. "You look like you've been through hell."

"Feel worse," Tory replied, her voice sharp. She didn't bother with small talk. "I need your help."

Antonio raised an eyebrow, a faint smirk playing on his lips. "Last time we talked, you said you'd rather walk into traffic than owe me a favor."

"Someone's trying to frame me for murder," Tory said, her tone clipped. "High-ranking syndicate, tied to Herrera. If you know anything—"

"I might," Antonio interrupted, swirling the amber liquid in his glass. "But what's in it for me?"

Tory's green eyes narrowed. "How about not getting dragged down with me? If I'm the target now, you're next."

Antonio's smirk faded, replaced by something colder. He studied her for a long moment before leaning forward.

"Fine," he said. "But if we're doing this, we do it my way."

Tory leaned back, her lips curving into a faint smile. "Wouldn't expect anything less."

The uneasy alliance was struck with little fanfare, but the weight of what lay ahead settled heavily on both of them.

For Tory, survival meant staying ahead of the lies—and trusting the one person who might have just as much to gain from her fall.

# CHAPTER 2
# UNEASY ALLIANCE

THE SMALL SAFE house in the Tenderloin was dim and claustrophobic, its peeling wallpaper and sagging furniture reeking of abandonment. Antonio Alvarez leaned against the kitchen counter, his dark eyes sharp and unreadable as he watched Tory pace the length of the room. The only light came from a single bare bulb swinging slightly overhead, casting shadows that shifted with her every movement.

"You're going to wear a hole in the floor," Antonio said, his voice smooth, tinged with faint amusement.

Tory shot him a glare, her green eyes alight with frustration. "You think this is funny? Someone just painted a target on my back and made sure everyone knows where to aim. And your name is probably next on their list."

Antonio shrugged, taking a slow sip from the chipped mug in his hand. "Then I'd better watch my back, shouldn't I?"

Her hands balled into fists at her sides. "Don't play coy with me, Antonio. You knew Herrera. You must've heard something—anything—that can explain why I'm being set up to take the fall for his murder."

Antonio placed the mug on the counter with deliberate care, his expression unchanging. "Let's say I do know something. How do I know I can trust you with it? You've got cops breathing down your neck, half the syndicate gunning for you, and the subtlety of a bull in a china shop."

Tory stopped pacing, her glare hardening. "If you didn't trust me at least a little, you wouldn't be here. So cut the crap and tell me what you know."

---

ANTONIO'S SILENCE stretched just long enough to make her wonder if he'd walk out. Then, with a faint sigh, he crossed the room and picked up a battered folder from the counter.

"Herrera wasn't just a lieutenant," he said, his voice low. "He was Junior Davos' eyes and ears in the city. Anything that passed through the syndicate, Herrera knew about it—and he knew how to make it work for Junior."

Tory frowned. "And now he's dead."

Antonio nodded. "Convenient for someone trying to shake up the power structure, wouldn't you say? Especially if they could pin it on an outsider."

Her mind raced, piecing together the implications. If someone had killed Herrera to disrupt Junior's hold on the syndicate, it wasn't just a random frame job—it was part of a larger game.

"And who do you think that someone is?" Tory asked, her tone sharp.

Antonio's mouth twitched into a knowing half-smile, his eyes remaining cold. "Now, that's the million-dollar question, isn't it?"

---

THE CONVERSATION SHIFTED as Antonio spread the folder's contents on the rickety table. Black-and-white surveillance photos, grainy but clear enough to show familiar faces, littered the surface. Among them was Herrera, seated at an outdoor café with several men Tory didn't recognize.

"Junior's been expanding his operations," Antonio explained, tapping one of the photos. "Drugs, weapons, high-end tech—he's dipping into everything. But there's been resistance. Some of the older factions don't like how reckless he's been, and Herrera was caught in the middle."

Tory studied the photos, her sharp eyes scanning for patterns. "So Junior's making enemies, and one of them decided to take him down a peg by killing Herrera."

"Maybe," Antonio said, though his tone was noncommittal. "Or maybe Junior saw Herrera as a liability and decided to clean house. Either way, it's messy, and you're smack in the middle of it."

Tory's jaw tightened. "And the frame job?"

Antonio shrugged. "That's the elegant part. Take you out, pin the chaos on you, and the real players get to keep their hands clean."

———

A FAINT NOISE outside caught Tory's attention. She moved to the window, parting the tattered curtain just enough to see the street below. A black sedan idled near the curb, its occupants hidden behind tinted windows.

"We've got company," she said, her voice low.

Antonio joined her, his gaze following hers. "Not cops. Syndicate muscle."

Tory's fingers brushed the pistol holstered beneath her jacket. "What do they want?"

Antonio's lips twisted into a sardonic smile. "To make sure you're not alive to prove them wrong."

———

THE FIRST KNOCK on the door was almost polite, a sharp contrast to the tension thickening the air. Antonio moved to the table, collecting the photos and slipping them back into the folder.

"You've got a plan, right?" Tory asked, her voice tight.

"Always," Antonio replied, his tone maddeningly calm.

The second knock came harder, followed by a voice muffled

through the door. "Wayne, we know you're in there. Open up, and maybe we'll make it quick."

Tory exchanged a glance with Antonio, her expression hardening. "I'll take the back."

He nodded, moving toward the front door. "I'll keep them busy."

---

TORY SLIPPED out the rear exit, her movements silent as she crept through the narrow alley behind the safe house. The frigid air bit at her skin, but she pushed the discomfort aside, her focus locked on the sounds of heavy boots approaching.

Antonio's voice carried faintly through the walls, smooth and mocking as he engaged the men at the front. Tory smirked despite herself. He had a way of irritating people that was almost admirable.

The alley opened onto the street, where another man waited—a burly figure leaning casually against the black sedan. Tory moved quickly, her pistol drawn but low.

"Hey!" the man barked, straightening as he spotted her.

Tory didn't wait. She closed the distance in three quick strides, her fist connecting with his jaw before he could react. He staggered, reaching for a weapon, but she followed up with a sharp kick to his knee that sent him sprawling.

"Sorry, buddy," she muttered, grabbing the keys from his pocket.

The shouts from the front of the house grew louder, punctuated by the crack of a gunshot. Tory slid into the driver's seat of the sedan, starting the engine with a roar.

"Antonio, move it!" she yelled, her voice carrying over the chaos.

---

THE FRONT DOOR burst open as Antonio sprinted toward the car, a sly grin breaking through his otherwise grim expression, undeterred by the bullet holes peppering the doorframe.

"Miss me?" he asked as he slid into the passenger seat.

"Not the time," Tory snapped, flooring the gas.

The sedan tore down the street, its tires screeching as Tory maneuvered through the narrow lanes. Behind them, a second car gave chase, its headlights blazing like twin spotlights in the dark.

"Got a plan for this too?" Tory asked, glancing at Antonio.

He reached into the glove compartment, pulling out a compact handgun. "Working on it."

---

THE CHASE LED them onto the freeway, the second car gaining ground as Tory weaved through sparse traffic. Antonio rolled down the window, leaning out just far enough to aim.

"Hold it steady," he muttered.

"Do I look like I'm trying to swerve?" Tory shot back.

The first shot shattered the other car's windshield, and the second sent it careening into the guardrail. Tory didn't wait to see the aftermath, pushing the sedan harder until the lights of the city faded into the distance.

---

THEY FINALLY STOPPED near the edge of the bay, the car idling as they caught their breath.

"Nice shooting," Tory said, her tone begrudging.

Antonio smirked, leaning back in his seat. "Nice driving."

Tory glanced at him, her expression hardening. "This isn't over, Alvarez. Whoever's pulling the strings won't stop until we're both dead."

Antonio's smirk faded, replaced by something colder. "Then we'd better find them first."

The uneasy alliance was cemented in silence as the bay's dark waters rippled around them.

# CHAPTER 3
# CRACKS IN THE SYNDICATE

THE NIGHTCLUB PULSED WITH LIFE, its pounding bass reverberating through the air and setting the rhythm for a world that never slept. Strobe lights flickered, casting fragmented shadows over the crowd that writhed and swayed on the dance floor. To anyone looking, this was just another Friday night in the city.

But Tory Wayne wasn't here to dance.

She slipped through the crowd, her sharp green eyes scanning the room as she adjusted the hem of her borrowed dress. The fabric clung to her in all the wrong places, a bold crimson that screamed for attention when she would have preferred to blend into the background.

"This is ridiculous," she muttered under her breath, her voice barely audible over the music.

Antonio Alvarez appeared at her side, his dark eyes flicking over the crowd with practiced ease. His tailored suit and easy smirk made him look like he belonged here, unlike Tory, who felt like a fish out of water.

"You look fine," he said, his voice smooth but amused. "Relax. You're supposed to be my date, not a walking threat assessment."

"Your date would probably be carrying a gun in her clutch," Tory shot back.

Antonio chuckled, motioning toward the VIP section on the second floor. "The people we're here to see don't take kindly to amateurs. So smile, look pretty, and try not to shoot anyone unless you absolutely have to."

---

THE VIP SECTION was a world away from the chaos below. Plush leather seating and glass tables replaced the sticky floors and strobing lights, and the low hum of conversation carried the weight of power and privilege.

At the center of it all sat Dominic Crane, a syndicate underboss with an iron grip on the city's drug trade. His broad shoulders and cold eyes gave him an intimidating presence, but it was the two men flanking him—Junior Davos' lieutenants—that made Tory's stomach twist.

Antonio leaned closer as they approached the table, his voice low. "Follow my lead. Crane's an opportunist, but he's loyal to whoever holds the most power. If Junior's losing his grip, Crane will be the first to notice."

"Good to know," Tory murmured.

Crane looked up as they arrived, his eyes narrowing slightly as he took them in. "Antonio Alvarez," he said, his voice gravelly. "Didn't think I'd see you back in my world. And with such charming company."

Antonio smirked, gesturing toward Tory. "This is Victoria. She's new to the scene but very interested in making the right connections."

Tory fought the urge to roll her eyes at the alias, instead offering Crane a polite smile. "It's a pleasure, Mr. Crane."

Crane's gaze lingered on her for a moment before he motioned for them to sit. "What brings you to my table, Antonio? Last I heard, you were keeping a low profile."

"Low profiles are overrated," Antonio replied, his tone light. "I'm here because I hear whispers. Rumors about cracks forming in the foundation. And I thought, who better to confirm or deny than the man who knows everything that moves in this city?"

Crane leaned back in his seat, his eyes gleaming with faint amusement. "Rumors are just that, Antonio. Stories people tell to make themselves feel important."

"Maybe," Antonio said, his smirk sharp. "But sometimes, rumors have teeth."Junior Davos sat at the head of the long mahogany table in the private room of his high-rise office. The room was sleek and sterile, devoid of the excess that his father preferred. Junior's style was modern efficiency—a direct reflection of how he ran his operations.

The men seated around him were silent, their postures rigid under his scrutinizing glare. They weren't used to his leadership style yet, and he liked it that way. Fear kept them sharp.

"Do you know what pisses me off the most?" Junior asked, his voice deceptively calm. He leaned back in his chair, twirling a gold pen between his fingers. "It's not the cops sniffing around. It's not even my father doubting me. It's the incompetence I see in this room."

He let the words hang in the air, his dark eyes scanning each man at the table. The pen stilled in his hand, and he tapped it against the surface once—twice—three times.

"Someone here," he continued, his tone colder now, "thought it would be a good idea to botch the Herrera situation. And now we have outsiders poking their noses where they don't belong."

One of the men shifted uncomfortably, his gaze darting to the others before settling back on Junior. "With respect, boss, we handled Herrera the way you wanted. The fallout—"

"Stop talking," Junior snapped, slamming the pen down. The sharp sound made the man flinch, and Junior's lip curled in disdain. "You think I care about your excuses? If I wanted to hear whining, I'd call my father."

The room fell silent again, tension thick enough to choke.

Junior stood, pacing slowly around the table. His movements were deliberate, each step a measured display of dominance. "Herrera was a pawn. Expendable. I told you to make it clean, and instead, you left a mess. Now Alvarez and that little cop are circling us like vultures."

He paused behind the man who had spoken earlier, resting a hand on his shoulder. The weight of it made the man visibly stiffen.

"If this happens again," Junior said softly, his voice carrying an edge of menace, "I'll make an example out of someone. And I promise you, it won't be pretty."

The man nodded quickly, swallowing hard. "Understood, boss."

Junior released his shoulder and returned to his seat, his expression calm once more. "Good. Now, let's talk about the freelancers. They're bringing in heat we don't need, but their precision can't be ignored. We'll use them for the big play next week, and then... we'll cut ties."

"What about Alvarez?" another man asked cautiously.

Junior smirked, leaning forward. "Alvarez thinks he's smart, but he's predictable. We'll deal with him when the time is right. For now, let him think he's one step ahead. The higher he climbs, the harder he'll fall."

The room murmured its agreement, but Junior wasn't listening anymore. His mind was already spinning with possibilities, each one bloodier than the last.

---

TORY LISTENED INTENTLY as Antonio and Crane danced around the subject, each testing the other's boundaries without giving away too much. The lieutenants watched silently, their expressions unreadable.

Finally, Crane's smirk faded. "If you're fishing for something, Alvarez, you'll have to be more specific. I don't have time for riddles."

Antonio's expression darkened slightly. "Junior Davos. Word on the street is he's getting reckless. Expanding too fast, stepping on toes. That kind of ambition tends to make enemies."

Crane's eyes flicked to his lieutenants before returning to Antonio. "Junior's got plenty of ambition, sure. But he's not stupid. He knows how to play the game."

"And Herrera?" Tory interjected, her tone sharp but measured. "Was he part of the game?"

The atmosphere shifted immediately. The lieutenants stiffened, and Crane's cold gaze locked onto her. "Interesting question for someone who's 'new to the scene.'"

Antonio placed a hand on Tory's arm, his grip firm but not aggressive. "Victoria's curious, that's all. She's heard the same whispers I have. Herrera's death didn't exactly go unnoticed."

Crane leaned forward, his elbows resting on the table. "Whispers can be dangerous, Antonio. Especially when they're about dead men. My advice? Let Herrera stay dead."

---

THE TENSION WAS palpable as they left the VIP section, the weight of Crane's warning lingering in the air. Tory walked slightly ahead, her fists clenched as she tried to process what they'd learned—or hadn't learned.

"That was a waste of time," she muttered, her frustration boiling over.

"Not entirely," Antonio said, catching up to her. "Crane didn't deny anything. That's as good as confirmation."

"Confirmation of what?" Tory snapped, turning to face him. "That Junior's making moves? That the syndicate's falling apart? None of that helps me figure out who framed me."

Antonio's dark eyes glinted, his quiet composure a deliberate provocation. "It's a start. And right now, starting's all we can do."

Tory shook her head, her green eyes blazing. "You're too comfortable with this, Antonio. Too willing to let things play out when we're running out of time."

Antonio's smirk faded, replaced by something colder. "Comfortable? You think I enjoy this? Watching the people I used to work with tear each other apart, knowing I'll never be able to walk away clean?"

Tory stepped closer, her voice low and sharp. "Then do something about it. Because if we don't figure this out soon, we're both going to end up like Herrera—dead and forgotten."

---

THE DRIVE back to the safe house was silent, tension filling the space between them like a tangible force. Antonio drove with his usual ease, but his grip on the wheel was tighter than usual. Tory stared out the window, her thoughts spinning as the city lights blurred past.

They had more questions than answers, but one thing was becoming increasingly clear: the cracks in the syndicate were widening, and Junior Davos was at the center of it all.

And Tory had a sinking feeling that the next crack would be aimed at her.

# CHAPTER 4
# BETRAYALS AND DEAD ENDS

THE RAIN CAME in sharp bursts as Tory Wayne moved through the narrow streets of Chinatown. The neon signs above flickered in the downpour, their bright reds and greens reflected in puddles that lined the uneven sidewalks. Tory kept her head low, the hood of her jacket pulled tightly around her face. Her breath fogged in the cool night air, every step measured and deliberate.

She felt it—the pressure of being watched. Whether it was police eyes, syndicate spies, or both, she couldn't be sure. But it didn't matter. She had a lead, and right now, it was the only thing keeping her moving.

Antonio's voice echoed in her mind: *"Crane isn't the only one who knows the syndicate's fractures. If you want answers, you'll find them closer to the cracks."*

Her destination was an unassuming herbal shop tucked between a dumpling house and a pawn shop. The faded red awning sagged under the weight of rainwater, and the gold lettering on the window was nearly illegible. To anyone else, it was just another storefront in a crowded street.

To Tory, it was a lifeline.

THE BELL above the door jingled softly as Tory stepped inside, shaking off the rain. The air was warm, thick with the mingling scents of dried herbs and incense. Shelves lined the walls, stocked with jars of powders and roots that glimmered faintly under the dim lights.

At the counter, a wiry man in his sixties looked up from a ledger. His sharp eyes softened slightly when they landed on Tory, but his expression remained cautious.

"You shouldn't be here," he said quietly, his hands still on the counter.

Tory pulled back her hood, a shadow of suspicion clouding her gaze. "I didn't have much of a choice, Lin. You said you'd call if you had anything."

Lin sighed, glancing toward the beaded curtain that led to the back of the shop. "And I told you that asking questions about the Davos family is dangerous. Herrera's death didn't just shake the syndicate—it's rattling the whole city."

Tory stepped closer, lowering her voice. "I'm already in the crosshairs. Someone wants me out of the picture, and they're using Herrera's murder to do it. If you know anything—"

Lin's sharp eyes darted toward the beaded curtain, his voice lowering as though the walls themselves were listening. "The cracks you're chasing aren't just fractures, Wayne. They're fault lines. Junior's not the worst of them—he's just the smoke. The fire's already burning, and it's bigger than you think."

Tory frowned, stepping closer. "What do you mean? Who's pulling the strings?"

Lin hesitated, his gaze flicking back to the counter as though weighing the risk of speaking. "Junior's deals aren't just with outsiders —they're with something… bigger. Something that doesn't care about San Francisco's old games."

Tory's chest tightened. "And what about me? Why frame me?"

Lin hesitated, his eyes flicking toward the front window. The sound of footsteps outside made him tense.

"They're watching," he whispered, his tone urgent. "You need to leave. Now."

THE FIRST THING Tory noticed as she stepped back into the rain was the black sedan parked at the curb. It wasn't there when she arrived.

Her pulse quickened as she scanned the street, catching sight of two figures stepping out of the car. Their suits were dark, their movements deliberate. Syndicate muscle—clean and professional.

Tory turned toward the alley, keeping her pace steady even as adrenaline coursed through her veins. She ducked into the narrow passage, the sound of the rain masking her footsteps.

But the moment she turned the corner, a third man blocked her path. His broad shoulders filled the alley, his scarred face twisting into a smirk as he stepped forward.

"Wayne," he said, his voice low and mocking. "Boss said you might show up here. Looks like tonight's my lucky night."

Tory's fingers brushed the grip of her pistol beneath her jacket. Her gaze flicked toward the fire escape above, quickly calculating the distance.

"Not feeling lucky," she said, her voice sharp.

The man's smirk widened as he raised his hand, motioning to the two figures closing in behind her. "Let's make this easy. You come with us, and maybe I'll let you walk out of this alive."

Tory didn't answer. She moved first.

THE PISTOL CAME out in one fluid motion, the silenced shot cutting through the rain as the man in front of her staggered back, clutching his shoulder.

Tory spun, firing twice more as the men behind her reached for their weapons. One dropped to the ground, groaning, while the other stumbled, blood staining his shirt.

She didn't wait to see if they recovered. She bolted for the fire escape, her boots splashing through puddles as she jumped and grabbed the ladder. The steel was cold and slick beneath her fingers as she hauled herself up, her breathing sharp and quick.

Shots rang out below, bullets ricocheting off the brick wall beside her. Tory pressed herself against the metal, her heart pounding as she climbed higher.

Reaching the rooftop, she rolled onto the wet surface, her pistol still in hand. The rain obscured her view of the alley below, but the sound of footsteps and shouted orders told her they weren't giving up.

---

SHE RAN.

The rooftops were uneven, their surfaces slick with rain and grime. Tory's boots slipped more than once, but she kept moving, jumping across narrow gaps and ducking beneath low pipes.

Behind her, the syndicate enforcers gave chase. Their footsteps echoed through the night, growing louder with every second.

Tory spotted a fire escape leading down to a quieter street and slid onto it, her movements quick but calculated. As she descended, she pulled out her phone, dialing the only number that mattered right now.

The line clicked.

"Alvarez," Antonio's voice came through, calm but alert.

"Antonio, I've got a tail," Tory said, her voice low but urgent. "Syndicate. Three of them."

"Where are you?"

"Chinatown. Near Lin's shop."

There was a brief pause. "Stay put. I'm on my way."

---

TORY REACHED THE STREET, her sharp eyes scanning for an escape route. She ducked into a small parking lot, her back pressed against a van as the rain continued to pour.

The enforcers were close, their voices carrying over the sound of the storm.

"She's here somewhere," one of them muttered.

Tory's grip on her pistol tightened. Her breathing steadied as she prepared for the inevitable.

The roar of an engine cut through the tension. A black car skidded into the lot, its headlights flooding the space as Antonio's voice called out.

"Get in!"

Tory didn't hesitate. She sprinted for the car, the enforcers shouting behind her as bullets pinged off the metal. She dove into the passenger seat, slamming the door as Antonio floored the gas.

---

THE CAR SPED through the rain-soaked streets, the enforcers' sedan in pursuit. Antonio's expression was calm, but his hands gripped the wheel tightly as he navigated the narrow lanes.

"Lin's shop?" he asked, his tone casual despite the chaos.

Tory nodded, her breath still coming in sharp bursts. "He had intel. Said Junior's working with outsiders, making deals that don't sit well with the old guard."

Antonio's lips curled into a wry smile. "Sounds about right. Anything else?"

"He said they're watching me. Everywhere."

Antonio's expression darkened. "Then you're not safe anywhere."

The chase ended abruptly when Antonio swerved onto a side street, the pursuing car skidding out on the slick pavement.

As the lights of the city faded into the distance, Tory leaned back in her seat, her green eyes hard.

"They're coming for me," she said quietly. "And they're not stopping until I'm dead."

Antonio glanced at her, his smirk faint but sharp. "Then let's make sure we get to them first."

# CHAPTER 5
# DIGGING UP TRUTHS

THE DINER in the Mission District had seen better days. Its faded sign flickered in the evening drizzle, and the air inside smelled of stale coffee and grease. But to Tory Wayne, the quiet hum of the old jukebox and the low murmur of a few scattered patrons made it the perfect meeting spot.

She sat in a booth near the back, her green eyes fixed on the rain streaking the window. Her hood was up, shadowing her face as she stirred the untouched cup of coffee in front of her.

Across from her, Antonio Alvarez leaned back casually, his dark eyes scanning the room. His suit was immaculate despite the damp night, and his smirk hadn't faltered since they arrived.

"How long are we supposed to wait?" Tory muttered, her voice low.

Antonio shrugged. "As long as it takes. Informants don't exactly keep a strict schedule."

Tory's fingers drummed against the table. "And you're sure this guy has something?"

"He's nervous," Antonio said, his tone calm. "Nervous people tend to know things worth hearing. Just don't spook him. He's not one of your cops; he doesn't scare so easily."

Tory shot him a look but didn't respond. She hated relying on Antonio's underworld connections, but she was out of options.

Tory leaned back against the vinyl seat, her gaze fixed on the rain streaking the diner's window. The patter of droplets on the glass seemed to echo her own swirling thoughts. She'd spent years chasing down criminals like Antonio, living by a black-and-white code that didn't leave much room for grey. But now, the lines between right and wrong felt as blurred as the world outside that rain-streaked pane.

Antonio wasn't just a lifeline—he was a risk. The kind of man who could switch sides in a heartbeat if it meant survival. Yet here she was, relying on his underworld connections, stepping deeper into a world she'd once sworn to dismantle.

She drummed her fingers against the edge of the table, her jaw tightening. Had she lost sight of what she was even fighting for? Every step further into this operation felt like another piece of herself slipping away, replaced by something colder, harder. Survival wasn't supposed to feel this compromising.

Her thoughts flicked back to her days as a cop—long nights in patrol cars, the steady rhythm of her partner's voice grounding her. Those memories felt like they belonged to someone else, a version of herself that wouldn't recognize the person she was becoming.

Tory shook herself, tearing her eyes from the window. The past was a luxury she couldn't afford. Right now, survival demanded that she trust Antonio. But some part of her still whispered that every step closer to him was another step into the dark.

---

THE INFORMANT ARRIVED ten minutes later, slipping through the door like he was trying to disappear before he'd even entered. He was thin and wiry, his eyes darting nervously as he approached their table.

Antonio gestured for him to sit, his smirk widening. "Relax, Carter. We're all friends here."

Carter didn't look convinced. He slid into the booth, his movements quick and jerky, like a bird preparing to take flight.

"You didn't say she'd be here," Carter muttered, his gaze flicking to Tory.

"She's the one asking the questions," Antonio replied smoothly.

Tory leaned forward, her voice sharp but steady. "And you're the one with the answers. Let's skip the small talk."

Carter hesitated, his hands fidgeting with the edge of the table. "I don't like this," he muttered.

"You don't have to like it," Tory said, her gaze narrowing. "You just have to talk. Start with Junior Davos."

---

CARTER GLANCED AROUND THE DINER, his paranoia palpable. "Junior's making moves—big moves. He's cutting deals with people outside the syndicate, bringing in weapons, drugs, tech...you name it. Stuff the old guard would never touch."

"Why the outsiders?" Antonio asked, his tone casual but pointed.

"Leverage," Carter replied. "Junior doesn't trust his own people. Too many of them still loyal to his father. He's building something new —something he can control."

Tory's jaw tightened. "And Herrera? Where does he fit into all this?"

Carter shifted uncomfortably. "Herrera was...complicated. He played both sides, kept Junior's enemies close. But Junior found out, and, well..."

Tory's heart sank. "Junior killed him?"

Carter shook his head quickly. "No, not directly. But he gave the order, or at least looked the other way. Thing is, someone else took advantage of it. Framed you to send a message—one that would shake the whole damn city."

"Who?" Tory demanded, her voice rising.

Carter hesitated again, his gaze darting to Antonio.

"Spit it out," Antonio said, his smirk fading.

Carter sighed. "There's a group—call them freelancers. They're the ones who actually pulled the trigger on Herrera. They don't answer to

Junior or the old guard. They're in this for themselves, and they're damn good at staying invisible."

Tory leaned back, her mind racing. "And now they're gunning for me."

Carter nodded reluctantly. "You're a loose end. Someone who could connect the dots if you dig deep enough."

---

THE SOUND of the door opening drew Carter's attention. His face paled as two men in dark jackets entered, their eyes scanning the room.

"We've got company," Carter whispered, his voice trembling.

Tory turned to look, her fingers instinctively brushing the pistol holstered beneath her jacket. Antonio's lips twitched upward, but his gaze remained sharp, dissecting the situation.

"Friends of yours?" he asked Carter.

Carter shook his head. "No, no, no...this wasn't part of the deal."

"Stay calm," Tory said, her voice low but firm. "They don't know anything yet."

The men moved closer, their eyes lingering on Carter before shifting to Tory and Antonio. One of them pulled a phone from his pocket, raising it like he was taking a picture.

Antonio moved first.

His hand shot out, grabbing the man's wrist and twisting it sharply. The phone clattered to the table as Antonio stood, his expression cold.

"Rude," he said, his voice deadly calm.

The second man reached for something beneath his jacket, but Tory was faster. Her pistol was out in an instant, the silencer in place as she aimed it directly at his chest.

"Don't," she warned, her tone icy.

The man froze, his eyes darting between Tory and Antonio.

"Time to go," Antonio said, pulling Carter to his feet.

---

THE THREE OF them slipped out the back of the diner, the rain masking their footsteps as they moved quickly down the alley. Tory kept her pistol low but ready, her sharp eyes scanning the shadows for signs of pursuit.

Carter was shaking, his breaths coming in sharp bursts. "This is bad—really bad. They'll know it was me."

"You knew the risks," Antonio said, his tone dismissive.

Carter glared at him but didn't argue.

They reached a parked car, and Antonio opened the door, shoving Carter inside. Tory slid into the passenger seat, her grip on her pistol tightening as Antonio started the engine.

"Where to?" she asked.

Antonio glanced at her, his smirk faint but steady. "Somewhere quiet. Carter and I need to have a chat."

---

THE DRIVE WAS TENSE, the rain streaking the windows as the city lights blurred into the distance.

"What now?" Tory asked, her voice sharp.

"Now," Antonio said, "we figure out who hired those freelancers—and why they want you out of the picture."

Tory's jaw tightened. "And if we can't?"

Antonio's smirk faded, replaced by something colder. "Then we make sure they don't get another chance."

Tory leaned back, her mind spinning. The pieces were coming together, but the picture they painted was darker than she'd imagined.

Junior's ambition, the freelancers' precision, and the tangled loyalties within the syndicate all pointed to one thing:

This wasn't just a power grab. It was a war—and Tory was caught in the crossfire.

# CHAPTER 6
# THE TRAP

THE ABANDONED PRECINCT WAS COLDER than Tory expected. The drafty halls whispered with the ghosts of its former life: faded crime scene photos pinned to corkboards, desks layered in dust, and the faint smell of mildew seeping through cracked walls.

It had been shuttered for over a decade, long forgotten by anyone who didn't know the city's underbelly. For Tory Wayne, it was the perfect place to regroup—and to confront the one person who could help her put the pieces together.

Antonio stood near a broken window, his silhouette outlined by the dim glow of a nearby streetlight. His usual smirk was absent, replaced by the hard expression of someone preparing for a fight.

"You sure about this?" he asked, his voice low.

Tory checked her pistol, the weight of it steady in her hand. "No. But we don't have a choice."

They had spent hours going through the names Carter had spilled, cross-referencing them against what little intel Antonio could provide. One name kept surfacing—a cop.

Sergeant Mike Callahan.

Tory had worked with him once, years ago. He was sharp, ambitious, and just slippery enough to stay ahead of internal affairs. If anyone had the reach to help frame her and the connections to the syndicate, it was him.

Antonio shifted, glancing toward the door. "He's not stupid. He'll know it's a setup."

Tory's green eyes flashed. "Good. Let him know. I want him nervous."

---

THE SOUND of footsteps echoed through the empty halls before the door creaked open. Callahan entered cautiously, his hand hovering near the service pistol at his side.

He was older now, the lines on his face deeper, his hair flecked with gray. But his sharp eyes hadn't dulled, and the way they flicked between Tory and Antonio told her he was already calculating his options.

"Wayne," he said, his voice calm but edged with suspicion. "This is...unexpected."

Tory stepped forward, her pistol lowered but ready. "Cut the crap, Callahan. You know why you're here."

Callahan's gaze lingered on Antonio. "This your new partner? Not exactly regulation."

Antonio's lips curled in a sardonic smile, his posture relaxed but watchful. "I'm more of a consultant."

"Enough," Tory snapped, her gaze sharpening. "You've been feeding intel to the syndicate, haven't you? Helping them frame me."

Callahan's expression didn't change, but the slight shift in his stance was enough to confirm her suspicion.

"I don't know what you're talking about," he said smoothly.

Tory raised her pistol, her voice cold. "Try again."

---

FOR A MOMENT, the room was silent except for the faint creak of the building settling. Then Callahan sighed, raising his hands slightly.

"Fine," he said, his tone laced with irritation. "I passed along some tips. It's not like I had a choice. You know how this city works, Wayne. You pick a side, or you get buried."

"Why me?" Tory demanded, her voice sharp. "Why frame me for Herrera?"

Callahan's eyes flicked to Antonio again, his smirk returning faintly. "You're a threat. Too smart, too stubborn, too nosy for your own good. Junior needed a scapegoat, and you were already halfway to the chopping block."

Tory's jaw tightened. "And you just went along with it."

"I survived," Callahan said simply.

---

THE SOUND of a distant car engine broke the tension. Antonio moved to the window, peering into the darkness.

"We've got company," he said, his voice calm but alert.

Callahan's smirk widened. "Guess they didn't trust me to handle this alone."

Tory grabbed him by the collar, slamming him against the wall. "What did you do?"

Callahan chuckled, his tone mocking. "You think Junior would leave me hanging? You're done, Wayne. Both of you."

Antonio turned, his pistol drawn. "We need to move."

Tory shoved Callahan back, her green eyes blazing. "Not until he talks. What's Junior planning?"

Callahan grinned, his teeth glinting in the dim light. "Wouldn't you like to know?"

---

THE FIRST GUNSHOT shattered the window, sending shards of glass scattering across the room. Antonio pulled Tory down as another shot ricocheted off the wall.

The first gunshot shattered the window, spraying shards of glass across the room like deadly confetti. The sharp, acrid scent of gunpowder filled the air, blending with the mildew that clung to the walls. Tory hit the ground hard as Antonio dragged her down, her ears ringing from the sharp crack of another bullet ricocheting off the filing cabinet behind them.

"They're not here to negotiate," Antonio muttered, his voice grim but steady.

Tory's pulse pounded in her ears. The cold floor pressed against her cheek as she crawled toward cover. Shards of glass bit into her palms, a sharp reminder of how exposed they were.

"Callahan!" she shouted over the chaos, her voice hoarse. "Get your ass behind something before they take it off!"

The older man scrambled behind a desk, his movements less agile than hers. Another bullet tore through the air, splintering the desk's edge.

"They're closing in," Antonio said, his pistol raised. He fired twice, the muzzle flashes lighting up the room like lightning strikes. The shadows outside the shattered windows shifted, figures moving with predatory precision.

Tory's green eyes darted to the exit. "We need to move. Now."

"Agreed," Antonio replied, his voice clipped.

The sound of rain hitting the roof intensified, masking the softer footfalls of their attackers. Tory gritted her teeth as she pushed herself up, every muscle in her body taut with adrenaline.

They darted toward the side corridor, Antonio covering their retreat with a few well-placed shots. The sharp scent of gunpowder clung to the air, mingling with the metallic tang of adrenaline in Tory's mouth.

A guard stepped into their path, his weapon raised. Tory didn't hesitate. Her shot was clean, the recoil biting into her shoulder as the man crumpled to the ground.

"Nice," Antonio said, sparing her a fleeting smirk.

"Save the compliments," she snapped, dragging Callahan along as they reached the back exit.

Antonio kicked the door open, and the cold night air hit them like a slap. The rain poured in sheets, drenching them instantly. The wet pavement gleamed under the faint glow of a nearby streetlight, the city's ever-present hum blending with the distant wail of a siren.

"Move!" Tory shouted, her voice barely audible over the downpour.

They sprinted down the alley, their footsteps splashing through puddles. The rain masked their movements, but it also made the terrain treacherous. Tory's boots slipped on the slick concrete, and Antonio caught her arm before she fell.

Callahan stumbled behind them, cursing under his breath. "This is insane—"

"Keep moving, or I'll leave you for them," Tory snapped, her green eyes blazing.

Antonio glanced over his shoulder, his dark eyes sharp. "Don't tempt her."

Bullets peppered the walls around them as they rounded a corner, the sound muffled by the relentless rain. Tory's lungs burned, every breath a struggle as she pushed herself forward. Finally, Antonio led them to the car he had stashed nearby—a battered sedan hidden beneath a tarp.

They piled in, the interior damp and musty. Antonio turned the ignition, and the engine roared to life.

"Hold on," he muttered, his hands tightening on the wheel.

The car fishtailed briefly as they sped into the street, neon lights streaking across the rain-slick windshield. Tory twisted in her seat, her pistol still drawn as she scanned for pursuers.

Callahan was hunched in the back, his face pale but defiant. "You'll never win this, Wayne. Junior's got an army."

Tory turned back, her voice ice-cold. "So do I."

They reached the back exit, where Antonio kicked the door open and stepped into the alley. The rain had returned, masking their footsteps as they moved toward the street.

Callahan stumbled, cursing under his breath. "You're wasting your time, Wayne. Junior's got people everywhere. You'll never—"

Tory spun, grabbing him by the arm. "Keep talking, Callahan. It's the only thing keeping you alive right now."

---

THE CAR ANTONIO had stashed nearby was old but reliable. They piled in, Tory shoving Callahan into the backseat as Antonio started the engine.

The streets blurred past in a haze of rain and neon lights as they drove, the tension in the car thick enough to choke.

"You've got a choice," Tory said, her voice sharp. "You tell us what Junior's planning, or I let Antonio handle you."

Callahan snorted. "He doesn't scare me."

Antonio's grin reflected darkly in the rearview mirror. "Give me five minutes. You'll be terrified."

---

BY THE TIME they reached the warehouse on the city's edge, Callahan was sweating. Tory pulled him out of the car, her grip like iron as she dragged him inside.

The empty space echoed with their footsteps as Antonio locked the door behind them.

"Start talking," Tory demanded, shoving Callahan into a chair.

Callahan hesitated, his eyes darting between them. "Junior's planning to wipe out the old guard—every last one of them. He's bringing in freelancers, hit squads, whatever it takes to take control. And you? You're just a bonus. A message to anyone who thinks about crossing him."

Tory's stomach twisted, but she kept her expression hard. "And the cops? How deep does this go?"

Callahan laughed bitterly. "Deep enough to bury you."

---

THE INFORMATION WAS DAMNING, but Tory knew it wasn't enough. Junior's network was vast, and the cracks in the syndicate were spreading faster than she'd anticipated.

As she and Antonio stepped outside, leaving Callahan tied up and cursing in the warehouse, Tory's mind raced.

"This isn't just about survival anymore," she said quietly.

Antonio lit a cigarette, his dark eyes glinting in the rain. "No. It's about taking control."

Tory nodded, her green eyes hard. "And taking Junior down."

# CHAPTER 7
# REVELATIONS AND ESCAPE

THE ABANDONED boathouse was quiet except for the rhythmic lapping of waves against the dock. Moonlight seeped through cracks in the wooden walls, casting fractured patterns across the floor. Tory Wayne stood in the shadows near a cluttered workbench, her trained gaze scanning the room.

Antonio Alvarez leaned casually against the doorframe, his pistol resting loosely in his hand. His calm demeanor belied the tension crackling in the air.

"Remind me why we're here again?" Antonio asked, his voice low but edged with impatience.

Tory didn't look at him. "Because Junior's planning something big, and if we don't get ahead of it, we're done."

Antonio arched a brow. "You say that like we're not already done."

Tory ignored him, her gaze flicking to the door. They'd arranged the meeting through one of Antonio's contacts—a risk, but a necessary one. If the informant had real intel on Junior's next move, it could change everything.

But they were cutting it close. Too close.

THE CREAK of a distant floorboard sent a jolt through Tory's nerves. Her hand hovered near her pistol as the door creaked open, revealing a wiry man in a dark jacket. His face was shadowed, but the tension in his posture was unmistakable.

"Glad you could make it," Antonio said, his tone smooth but watchful.

The man nodded, stepping inside and glancing around nervously. "This place isn't exactly secure."

"It's secure enough," Tory said, her voice sharp. "What do you have?"

The man hesitated, his eyes flicking to the corners of the room. "Junior's planning a hit. Big one. He's targeting the old guard—every major player who still answers to his father. He wants them out of the way, and he's bringing in outside help to make sure it's clean."

Tory's stomach tightened. "When?"

"Tomorrow night," the man said. "Big meeting downtown, neutral territory. Junior's people will be there, and so will the freelancers. It's going to be a bloodbath."

The man hesitated, glancing nervously at Antonio before leaning in closer to Tory. His voice dropped to a whisper, barely audible over the faint creak of the boathouse. "But it's not just Junior calling the shots anymore. There's someone else. Bigger."

Tory frowned. "What do you mean?"

"They call it The Veil," the man said, his face pale. "I don't know much—no one does—but they're the ones pulling the strings behind the freelancers. Junior's just a pawn to them. They're letting him think he's in control, but when the time comes…" He trailed off, his hands trembling.

Antonio leaned back, his expression unreadable. "The Veil? Sounds like a ghost story. Convenient excuse to keep people scared."

The man shook his head violently. "It's not a story. It's real. They've got connections everywhere—politics, law enforcement, even outside the country. If Junior succeeds, it's because they let him. And if he fails…" He shivered, looking away.

Tory exchanged a glance with Antonio, unease settling in her gut. "Why haven't we heard about them before?"

"Because they don't leave trails," the man said. "And if they find out I told you this..." He didn't finish, but the fear in his eyes said enough.

Antonio's lips curved, a chilling contrast to the glint of calculation in his eyes. "Good thing we're all friends here, right?"

Tory ignored him, leaning in closer to the informant. "What do they want?"

"I don't know," he admitted, his voice barely above a whisper. "But whatever it is, it's bigger than Junior. Bigger than all of us."

Antonio raised an eyebrow. "And you're just handing us this out of the goodness of your heart?"

The man smirked faintly. "Let's just say I don't like how Junior's running things. He's reckless. Dangerous. The old guard has rules— Junior doesn't care about rules."

Tory leaned forward, her green eyes hard. "Where's the meeting?"

"An old ballroom on Market Street. No windows, tight security. If you're thinking about crashing it, you're suicidal."

---

THE SOUND of tires crunching gravel outside cut the conversation short. Antonio moved to the window, his sharp eyes narrowing.

"We've got company," he muttered.

The informant paled. "I didn't tell anyone—"

"Doesn't matter," Tory snapped. "They're here now."

---

THE FIRST GUNSHOT shattered the boathouse's fragile quiet. Tory ducked behind the workbench as bullets splintered the wooden walls. Antonio returned fire, his pistol barking sharply in the confined space.

The informant scrambled toward the door, panic written across his face.

"Don't—" Tory started, but it was too late.

The man stepped into the open and went down in a hail of bullets, his body collapsing against the dock.

"Damn it!" Tory hissed, her grip tightening on her pistol.

Antonio moved beside her, his expression grim. "We need to move."

---

THE BACK EXIT led to a narrow dock that stretched out over the water. Tory and Antonio moved quickly, their footsteps muffled by the sound of waves.

"They're closing in," Antonio said, glancing over his shoulder.

Tory spotted a small motorboat tied to the dock. "That'll do."

They climbed in, Tory fumbling with the ropes while Antonio started the engine. The boat roared to life, its motor cutting through the night as they sped away from the boathouse.

Bullets ricocheted off the water around them, but the distance grew quickly, the shouts of their pursuers fading into the night.

---

BY THE TIME they reached the safety of a nearby cove, Tory slumped against the edge of the boat, her pistol still in hand. The cold spray of the bay stung her cheeks, cutting through the fading adrenaline. Her green eyes stayed fixed on the dark horizon, but her thoughts churned with the chaos of the ambush.

Antonio leaned back, lighting a cigarette with practiced ease. His hands were steady, but his silence betrayed something else—calculation.

"Well," he said, finally breaking the quiet, "that went about as smoothly as a gunfight in a barn."

Tory shot him a withering look but didn't reply.

Antonio exhaled a plume of smoke, his dark eyes flicking toward her. "You still planning on crashing Junior's little soirée?"

Tory didn't answer right away. Her fingers brushed the damp surface of her phone in her jacket pocket, replaying the informant's final words in her mind: *The Veil... Junior's just a pawn.*

"We have to," she said finally, her voice steady despite the storm in her chest. "If we don't, the old guard's dead, and this city belongs to Junior—and whoever's pulling his strings."

Antonio's smirk faded, replaced by a sharp, unreadable expression. "Fine. But if you're planning to go against The Veil, you'd better know what you're walking into. Ghost stories have teeth, Wayne."

Tory turned toward him sharply. "And how do you know so much about them?"

Antonio's gaze didn't waver, but his smirk returned, colder this time. "I keep my ear to the ground. Doesn't mean I've seen them."

Tory wanted to press, but a flicker of doubt gave her pause. Antonio was an expert at deflection, and the timing of their ambush wasn't sitting right with her.

Her phone buzzed in her pocket, cutting through her thoughts. She pulled it out, her breath catching as she read the message:

*"You're compromised. Watch your back."*

Her pulse quickened, and her eyes snapped to Antonio. He didn't seem to notice—or maybe he was just that good at pretending.

"Who's that?" Antonio asked, his tone casual.

"No one," Tory said, slipping the phone back into her pocket. But her mind raced.

The timing, the ambush, and now this warning—something didn't add up. If Junior's freelancers had infiltrated her network, she was in more danger than she'd realized. And if Antonio had tipped them off…

Tory's jaw tightened. She'd deal with Junior and his freelancers, but if Antonio was playing both sides, he wouldn't get a second chance.

The boat's engine roared back to life, carrying them toward the faint glow of the city. As the skyline grew closer, so did the weight of her resolve.

Junior's party was only the beginning. The Veil was watching, and now, so was she.

The End

# VEILED

## A SHORT THRILLER

# CHAPTER 1
# INTO THE WEB

THE CHANDELIER above blazed like a constellation of fractured stars, its cold brilliance scattering shards of light onto the polished marble below. Tory Wayne adjusted the shimmering mask over her face, each flick of her fingers deliberate, as though rehearsing a well-worn role. Her vintage silver dress clung to her like a whisper of smoke, shimmering with every step she took. It wasn't just a dress; it was a weapon, the final layer of a disguise designed to disarm.

Beneath the dazzling façade of San Francisco's elite, Tory was a predator, her sharp green eyes catching everything as she moved through the crowd. Her steps were unhurried, her posture languid, but her mind worked like a machine, categorizing and calculating every face, every word, every angle. The stakes were too high to miss even the smallest detail.

The penthouse, perched atop one of the city's tallest skyscrapers, was a palace in the sky, its soaring windows offering a breathtaking panorama of San Francisco's endless lights. For most of the guests, the view was a symbol of wealth and power. To Tory, it was camouflage. The true theater of this night wasn't the dazzling skyline but the smaller stage of whispered conversations and fleeting glances, exchanged in the shadows of this glittering crowd.

Near the far end of the room, clusters of men in tailored suits and jewel-tone gowns gathered, their chatter overlapping with the sound of clinking glasses and the murmur of live strings. Tory swept her gaze across the gathering, taking in the room's energy like an actor scanning a stage before a performance. She adjusted one of her diamond-studded earrings, the delicate piece doubling as a listening device, its technology as refined as it was discreet. The ambient noise of laughter and clinking glasses filled her ears, but her training allowed her to filter through it, isolating voices worth hearing.

Her eyes landed on Antonio Alvarez, lounging against the marble bar like he owned the place. His black suit was so perfectly tailored it looked effortless—though Tory knew better. Antonio never did anything by accident. Even the slightly loosened tie was part of his act, the perfect balance of debonair charm and dangerous swagger. His smile, fleeting and sharp, was the sort that invited trust just long enough for him to break it.

He caught her eye and raised his glass in a mock toast. Tory met his gaze but didn't react. Antonio's smirk deepened as though her lack of response was exactly what he expected. No matter where she went, Antonio was always there—a player in the same game, but with rules only he seemed to understand.

Tory shifted her focus, letting the noise of the room wash over her as she resumed her silent hunt. Her target wasn't Antonio, tempting as it might have been to pin down his elusive motives. No, tonight was about information. This fundraiser—one of Junior Davos's many calculated plays to network with power—was an opportunity-rich minefield, and Tory intended to walk it without so much as a misstep.

The guests were a who's who of influence: politicians, corporate titans, and underworld figures hiding behind carefully polished veneers. They mingled freely, their polite laughter hiding the tangled webs of corruption and betrayal that truly connected them. Tory didn't just want names; she needed leverage—knowledge of the unseen strings tying these people to Junior's empire.

As she moved, her sharp eyes caught on a pair of men standing near the balcony. They weren't the most obvious targets—dressed too sharply to be muscle, too stiff to be seasoned players—but something about their body language caught her attention. Their heads were close, their movements tense, as though every word exchanged carried weight.

Tory adjusted the strap of her dress, her movements graceful but calculated, and sidled closer to the balcony. Her listening device crackled faintly, syncing to their voices over the noise.

"...shifting alliances," one of them murmured, his voice clipped. "Junior's too volatile. If The Veil thinks he's an asset, they're making a mistake."

The second man, older and slightly stooped, with an aura of weariness that spoke to years of secrets, nodded grimly. "You think The Veil cares about Junior's stability? He's a pawn—one they'll discard the second he stops being useful."

Tory's pulse quickened. The Veil. Even among those who trafficked in whispers and shadows, their name carried a rare kind of weight. Few understood who—or what—they truly were, but their influence was undeniable, woven into the very fabric of the city's power structure.

As the men spoke, a single phrase stood out like a beacon: a shipment tied to The Veil. Tory strained to catch more, her grip tightening on the sleek black clutch in her hand. The right details about this shipment could be the thread she needed to unravel the web.

"Excuse me, miss."

The voice, smooth but edged with steel, cut through her focus like a blade. Tory turned slowly, her muscles taut as a bowstring. A man in a perfectly tailored black suit stood behind her, his angular features highlighted by the chandelier's unforgiving light. His dark eyes locked onto hers, sharp and searching.

"Have we met?" he asked, his voice polite but carrying an undertone of suspicion.

Tory tilted her head, a slow, practiced smile curving her lips. "I don't believe so. Though... I feel like I've seen you before." Her voice was light, a little playful, but never careless.

The man frowned, his gaze narrowing. "I don't recall."

Her instincts screamed a warning. This wasn't idle curiosity; he was testing her. The seconds stretched, every beat a chance for suspicion to harden into certainty.

"Oh, my mistake," she said, letting a soft laugh escape. "It must have been someone else. My apologies." Tory made to turn, but the man's hand shot out, catching her arm in a grip that was firm enough to make a point without causing a scene.

"Wait."

Her pulse thundered in her ears, drowning out the noise of the crowd. Slowly, she turned back, arching a brow at him. "Yes?"

"You don't belong here," he said, his voice lowering to a near growl.

Tory met his gaze head-on, her practiced smile not faltering. "Oh? And you do?"

His eyes flickered, but his grip didn't loosen. "More than you might think," he said, his tone colder now. Then, releasing her arm, he straightened his jacket. "It would be a shame for anyone to cause... unnecessary trouble tonight."

Her smile sharpened. "Trouble's only an issue if you're unprepared for it. But I'll take your advice under consideration."

Before the man could respond, a loud crash near the bar snapped both their attention. A tray of glasses shattered against the floor, and a waitress stammered apologies as guests turned to stare. Tory didn't hesitate. As his focus shifted, she slipped into the crowd, her steps measured but quick.

The tension in her chest eased slightly as she neared the ballroom's edge. A gilded door led to a quieter hallway, and she pushed through it, letting the heavy door close behind her.

Leaning against the wall, she exhaled slowly, forcing her breathing to even out. Her every nerve screamed to keep moving, but she couldn't afford haste. Haste got people killed.

The door creaked open. Tory's hand moved to the blade concealed beneath her dress, her breath catching. She relaxed—slightly—when Antonio stepped into the hall.

"You're slipping," he said, his voice low.

# CHAPTER 2
# SHADOWS AND SECRETS

THE SAFE HOUSE wasn't much to look at—a forgotten relic of another era, with peeling wallpaper curling like dead leaves and furniture sagging under decades of neglect. The faint, ever-present scent of mildew clung to the air, made heavier by the rain seeping through the cracked window frame. The single lamp on the kitchen table flickered erratically, its weak glow casting jittery shadows that twisted and stretched across the cracked plaster walls.

Tory Wayne leaned against the counter, her arms crossed tightly over her chest as Antonio Alvarez spread out a map and a stack of photographs on the wobbly table. Despite the room's oppressive gloom, Antonio's casual demeanor made it seem like he was hosting a poker game instead of outlining a plan that could get them both killed.

"These faces," Antonio began, his tone clipped as he tapped one of the grainy black-and-white photos with the back of his knuckles, "aren't just Junior's benefactors—they're his insurance policy. Politicians, police chiefs, corporate players. Each one's tied to him by dirty money or blood, and they've got plenty to lose if Junior burns."

Tory stepped closer, her green eyes narrowing as she studied the photos. The grainy images were damning: a police commissioner caught mid-handshake with a syndicate operative, a judge sipping champagne alongside Junior at an exclusive party, a tech CEO photographed leaving a private meeting with a man who specialized in black-market arms deals.

"And The Veil?" she asked, her voice sharp enough to cut through the room's stale air. "How do they fit into all this?"

"They don't 'fit,'" Antonio snapped, his irritation slipping through. "They're the architects, Tory. They don't prop up guys like Junior—they create them. These names?" He gestured to the photos spread across the table. "They're placeholders. Replaceable. Junior's just another piece on the board, and he's not even a knight. He's a pawn."

Tory leaned over the table, her fingers brushing the edge of one photo. "And what about The Veil's endgame? What's all this building toward?"

Antonio smirked, but it was a bitter, humorless thing. "Control," he said simply. "The Veil doesn't deal in messy power grabs or public displays. They make the rules, stack the deck, and let everyone else fight over the scraps. That way, no one notices they've already won."

The words settled like a weight on Tory's chest. She stared at the photos again, her sharp eyes scanning every detail. The truth was worse than she'd imagined. Junior wasn't the head of the snake—he was a distraction. The real danger lay in the hands of the invisible puppet masters, the ones pulling strings so expertly that most people didn't even know they were dancing.

Antonio reached into his leather satchel and pulled out a battered folder. Inside were even more damning documents: bank statements linking legitimate businesses to shell corporations, surveillance photos, and coded communications. Tory's breath hitched as she flipped through the papers.

"They're everywhere," Antonio continued, his voice low but laced with urgency. "Politics, law enforcement, city planning, tech—you name it. The Veil's got their hooks in every major sector. Taking them down isn't just about cutting off the head of the syndicate. It's about ripping out the spine of an entire system."

Tory swallowed hard, her stomach knotting. She'd always known San Francisco was a city built on compromise and corruption, but this? This was a cancer, its roots stretching deeper than she'd ever imagined.

Her gaze fell on a photo of a woman in a sharp tailored suit. Recognition hit like a punch to the gut. District Attorney Rachel Hargrove—someone Tory had once trusted, back when she still believed the law could solve problems. Back when she'd worn a badge. Hargrove had been one of the good ones, or so Tory had thought. Seeing her face now, tied to The Veil's shadowy network, felt like betrayal sharpened to a razor's edge.

"Is anyone clean anymore?" Tory muttered, her voice barely audible.

Antonio let out a low chuckle, but it was devoid of humor. "You're in the wrong city if you're looking for saints."

The tension between them was palpable as they sifted through the evidence. Antonio kept up his usual sardonic tone, throwing out the occasional quip, but Tory wasn't buying it. His evasiveness was as obvious as the cracks in the plaster walls.

"Where did you get all this?" she asked, holding up one of the reports.

Antonio's dark eyes flicked up briefly, his expression unreadable. "Does it matter?"

"Yes," Tory snapped, her frustration boiling over. "This isn't street-level intel. These are bank records, surveillance photos, *classified reports*. Someone high up handed you this. Who?"

Antonio leaned back in his chair, folding his arms across his chest. "You really want to know?"

Tory's eyes blazed. "I'm risking my life for this. Damn right, I want to know."

Antonio sighed, raking a hand through his hair. For the first time, his usual smirk faltered. "If I told you this came from someone inside The Veil—someone who's just as dirty as the rest of them—what then? Would it matter? Would you stop?"

Tory's jaw clenched. "I need to know who I'm dealing with."

Antonio hesitated, his gaze dropping to the folder in front of him. His voice, when he spoke, was quieter but no less firm. "Trust me on this, Tory. You don't want their name. Knowing it won't help—it'll just put a bigger target on your back."

Her fingers tightened around the edge of the table, frustration coursing through her veins. "You're deflecting," she said through gritted teeth.

"And you're pushing," Antonio retorted, his tone sharp. "Careful, Wayne. You might not like what you find."

The room fell silent, the air between them heavy with unspoken tension. Tory turned away, her grip tightening on the counter as she tried to rein in her anger. Antonio was hiding something big—something that could blow this operation wide open.

Finally, she spoke, her voice low but steady. "If we're going to take down The Veil, I need to know who's feeding you intel. Otherwise, we're flying blind."

Antonio leaned forward, his voice dropping to a near whisper. "And what if the person feeding me this is already working against you? What then?"

Tory stared at him, her sharp green eyes searching his face for any crack in his carefully crafted mask. "Then I'd still take them down. But at least I'd know the risks."

Before Antonio could respond, the sound of a car pulling up outside shattered the quiet. Tory moved to the window, parting the curtain just enough to see. A sleek black sedan idled at the curb, its windows tinted to a mirror sheen.

"We've got company," she said, her voice tight.

Antonio joined her, his expression hardening. "Syndicate muscle," he muttered. "Junior's boys. They're making their move."

A sharp knock on the door sent Tory's pulse racing.

"Tory Wayne," a smooth, venomous voice called from the other side. "Open up, and maybe we'll make this quick."

Another knock followed, harder this time, rattling the peeling doorframe.

Tory exchanged a glance with Antonio. "What's the play?"

His smirk returned, maddeningly calm. "You go out the back. I'll keep them busy."

"Not happening," Tory shot back.

"You're stubborn. I like that." His smirk widened. "But I'm not asking."

# CHAPTER 3
# TESTING LOYALTIES

THE OLD COURTHOUSE LOOMED AHEAD, its towering columns casting long, jagged shadows as the last rays of sunlight bled behind the horizon. The structure had once stood as a symbol of justice, but now it felt like a mausoleum—cold, empty, and haunted by too many compromises. Tory Wayne lingered in the alley across the street, her sharp green eyes scanning the area for signs of surveillance.

San Francisco's streets were deceptive that way. Even the most mundane settings could become stages for betrayal. The courthouse, with its crumbling grandeur, was no exception.

Her meeting tonight was with Judge Eleanor Blackwell—a name once synonymous with integrity. Blackwell had been a stalwart of the city's justice system, presiding over cases that defined the city's fragile morality. But power had a way of corrupting even the best, and whispers of Blackwell's dealings with The Veil had turned her once-pristine reputation into something murky. The judge's message to Tory had been succinct, almost cryptic:

**"Meet me at the courthouse. Midnight. We need to talk."**

Tory had debated whether to show up at all. Blackwell could be an ally, or she could be setting a trap. The only thing Tory was certain of was the risk.

A faint drizzle clung to her leather jacket, the cold beads sliding down the worn material as she kept her position in the shadows. Her mind worked tirelessly, cycling through scenarios. If this was a setup, how would it play out? Would The Veil send assassins, or had Blackwell already sold her out to Junior's goons? And if the judge was being sincere, what exactly had pushed her to reach out?

Tory's gaze drifted back to the courthouse. Its windows stared back at her, dark and hollow, like the sockets of a skull. Her thoughts turned to Blackwell's career, each detail sharpening her suspicion. The judge had once been a symbol of unshakable integrity, the kind of figure Tory had looked up to back when she was still a cop. But something had changed—fear, greed, or ambition had warped Blackwell into someone unrecognizable. The question now was whether the judge could still be salvaged—or if she was just another piece on The Veil's board.

"Second thoughts?"

The voice startled Tory just enough to make her hand twitch toward the concealed knife at her hip. She turned sharply to see Antonio Alvarez leaning against the damp brick wall behind her. His dark leather jacket and jeans gave him a rougher edge tonight, but the easy confidence in his posture was the same. Even dressed down, Antonio moved like he belonged everywhere and nowhere.

"Not second thoughts," Tory replied, her tone clipped. "Just weighing the odds."

Antonio smirked, the dim light catching the faint gleam of amusement in his dark eyes. "And what do they say?"

"She's dirty," Tory said, her voice even. "The question is whether she's dirty enough to help me—or dirty enough to sell me out."

Antonio pushed off the wall, his expression turning serious. "If Blackwell's tied to The Veil, she's playing a game you don't know the rules to."

Tory shot him a pointed look. "You think I don't know that? This isn't my first rodeo, Antonio."

He raised his hands in mock surrender, his smirk returning. "Fair enough. Just don't get too comfortable. The moment you think you've got someone like Blackwell figured out is the moment they pull the rug out from under you."

Tory didn't bother responding. Antonio's penchant for cryptic warnings was irritating, but she couldn't entirely dismiss him.

"I'll be close," Antonio added, stepping back into the shadows. "Call if you need backup."

And then he was gone, melting into the darkness as though he'd never been there.

---

THE COURTHOUSE DOORS groaned as Tory pushed them open, their heavy weight a testament to the building's age and neglect. Inside, the air was damp and stale, carrying the faint tang of disinfectant that failed to mask something more primal—something metallic and faintly sour, like dried blood long since scrubbed from the floors.

Flickering fluorescent lights buzzed faintly, casting uneven light across the cracked walls and worn carpet. Dust motes swirled lazily in the air, tiny ghosts of forgotten cases and fractured promises.

Tory moved cautiously, her footsteps muted against the fraying carpet as she navigated the shadowy halls. Her hand hovered near the pistol concealed beneath her jacket, every sense tuned to her surroundings.

When she reached the judge's chambers, the door was slightly ajar. Tory's stomach tightened as she nudged it open, her movements careful and deliberate.

Inside, Judge Eleanor Blackwell sat behind an imposing oak desk. She looked smaller than Tory remembered, her thin frame dwarfed by the towering bookshelves and heavy furniture of her office. The judge's silver hair was pulled back into a severe bun, and her piercing blue eyes met Tory's with an intensity that betrayed both resolve and exhaustion.

"You're punctual," Blackwell said, her voice low and even.

"You didn't leave much room for questions," Tory replied, taking the seat across from her.

Blackwell leaned forward, resting her elbows on the desk. The lines on her face seemed deeper in the dim light, etched by years of compromises and quiet battles. "You're in deep, Ms. Wayne. Deeper than you realize."

Tory arched a brow, her lips curving into a faint smirk. "Why don't you enlighten me?"

Blackwell's gaze didn't waver. "Junior Davos is reckless, but he's predictable. His ambition will burn him out eventually. The real threat isn't him—it's The Veil. They're moving pieces on the board you haven't even seen yet."

Tory's muscles tensed, but her expression remained neutral. "And you're tied to them, aren't you?"

Blackwell's shoulders stiffened slightly, the faintest flicker of guilt crossing her face. "I've had dealings with them," she admitted, her voice tight. "But not by choice. They're like a disease. Once they touch your life, there's no cure."

"So why call me?" Tory asked, leaning back in her chair. "What's your angle, Judge?"

Blackwell's fingers tightened around a pen on her desk, the plastic creaking under the pressure. "Because they've gone too far. They're consolidating power, and if Junior gets what he's after, the city won't just suffer—it'll collapse."

Tory studied the woman carefully, watching for cracks in her carefully constructed façade. For a brief moment, something raw surfaced —guilt, fear, or maybe desperation.

"You don't understand what they're capable of," Blackwell said, her voice barely above a whisper. "The Veil doesn't just buy people— they own them. Every decision I've made, every case I've ruled on... it's all been under their thumb."

Tory's jaw tightened. "And you think helping me clears your conscience?"

Blackwell's eyes flashed with anger. "I'm not doing this for absolution. I'm doing it because someone needs to stop them, and I can't do it alone."

The judge's words hung in the air, heavy with implication.

Tory exhaled slowly, crossing her arms. "What do you want in return?"

Blackwell met her gaze steadily. "Leave me out of it. I'll give you everything you need—names, locations, contacts—but my family stays protected."

Tory's green eyes narrowed. "You want to burn The Veil while keeping your hands clean. How noble."

Blackwell's expression hardened. "Don't lecture me, Ms. Wayne. You think you're above this? You think your hands are clean?"

The words hit harder than Tory cared to admit, but she refused to let it show.

"I'll take what you've got," Tory said, rising from her seat. "But if you're lying—or if this is a setup—you'll regret it."

Blackwell didn't flinch. "Just don't waste what I give you. The Veil doesn't leave second chances."

---

OUTSIDE, the courthouse loomed behind Tory like a stone monument to broken promises. Antonio was waiting under a streetlamp, his arms crossed.

"Well?" he asked, his voice casual.

"She gave me intel," Tory said, her tone clipped. "Names, places, connections. Enough to hurt The Veil—if it's legit."

"And the catch?"

"She wants to stay out of the crossfire," Tory said, glancing back at the courthouse.

Antonio smirked faintly. "Figures. You believe her?"

Tory hesitated. "I believe she's scared. But scared people are dangerous."

Antonio's smirk widened. "Then you'd better move fast, Wayne. The Veil doesn't leave loose ends."

A chill ran through Tory, but she masked it with a wry smile. "Neither do I."

As they disappeared into the night, her phone buzzed. A single message lit up the screen:

**"Careful who you trust. Blackwell isn't the only one watching."**

Tory's grip tightened on the phone. The game had just gotten even more dangerous.

# CHAPTER 4
# FACTIONS RISING

THE WAREHOUSE REEKED OF OIL, rust, and the faint metallic tang of something sharper—blood, or the kind of fear that never really leaves a place. Towering stacks of crates rose unevenly, casting jagged shadows that stretched into the darkness like skeletal fingers. The dim, flickering light from a row of dusty overhead lamps barely illuminated the cavernous space, creating a labyrinth of narrow corridors where sound seemed to vanish into the walls.

Outside, the low rumble of forklifts and the occasional clang of metal echoed faintly, a stark contrast to the suffocating stillness inside. Tory Wayne crouched low behind a stack of crates near the rear wall, her sharp green eyes darting between the shadows, every creak of the floorboards a potential threat. She had learned long ago that silence was rarely empty—it always carried the promise of something waiting to strike.

Antonio Alvarez was beside her, his posture relaxed despite the tension in the air. He glanced at her, his dark eyes gleaming with their usual mix of amusement and irritation. "You know, normal people let others handle suicide missions like this," he murmured.

Tory shot him a glare, her voice low but firm. "If you wanted normal, you wouldn't have followed me."

Antonio smirked, leaning back slightly against the crate. "Fair point. But you're still playing with fire."

She didn't respond, her attention fixed on the scene unfolding in the center of the warehouse. A dozen men stood in a loose circle, their tense postures and hushed voices betraying the volatility of the situation. At the center of it all was Junior Davos, his lean frame clad in a sharp gray suit that was as meticulously tailored as it was ill-suited to his company.

"Junior's putting on a show," Antonio murmured, his voice barely audible over the faint hum of machinery outside. "That smile's not for them—it's for himself."

Tory nodded, her gaze narrowing. "He's losing them. He knows it, and they know it."

Junior's voice cut through the warehouse like a blade, cold and commanding. "Let's make one thing clear: I'm not here to negotiate. If you're not with me, you're against me."

He swept his sharp gaze over the assembled lieutenants, his smirk faint but dangerous. It wasn't the casual grin of a man in control—it was the brittle edge of someone forcing himself to hold it together. As he adjusted the cuffs of his suit jacket with a practiced flourish, Tory caught the flicker of uncertainty in his eyes, quickly buried beneath the mask of confidence.

"I've bled for this syndicate," Junior continued, his voice steady but laced with menace. "I've done things most of you wouldn't survive, let alone understand. Don't mistake my ambition for recklessness. Everything I've built—everything *we've* built—depends on us staying ahead. If you can't stomach that, there's the door."

The silence that followed was heavy, the air thick with unspoken tension. No one moved. Tory could almost hear the crackle of unease rippling through the group.

Finally, one of the lieutenants, a burly man with a scar running the length of his jaw, stepped forward. His movements were slow, deliberate, each step a challenge. "You're overreaching, Junior," he said, his gravelly voice cutting through the quiet like a growl. "You think power is about taking what you want. But every move you make steps on the wrong toes. Keep pushing, and you'll get us all killed."

Junior's smirk widened, but there was no warmth to it. "Funny," he said, his tone light but dripping with venom. "I was just about to say the same thing."

Before the scarred lieutenant could respond, the crack of a gunshot shattered the silence. The sound was deafening in the enclosed space, echoing off the walls like a thunderclap.

Tory flinched as the lieutenant staggered backward, clutching his shoulder, blood seeping through his fingers. Junior lowered his pistol with practiced ease, his face a mask of cold fury.

"Let me make this clear," he said, his voice cutting through the stunned silence. "I don't negotiate with cowards. I eliminate them."

The lieutenant groaned, sinking to his knees as the others looked on, their expressions a mix of fear and barely concealed anger.

Junior's gaze swept over the group, daring anyone to defy him. "Now," he said, his tone hard as steel, "does anyone else have something to say?"

The silence that followed was absolute, the oppressive kind that made even breathing feel like a risk. Tory's fingers brushed the handle of her pistol, her muscles coiled like a spring. Antonio placed a hand on her arm, his touch firm but restrained.

"Not yet," he whispered, his voice barely audible.

Tory swallowed hard, forcing herself to stay still as Junior gestured to one of his men. A wiry figure emerged from the shadows, dragging a bound and gagged man into the circle. The captive's face was bruised and swollen, his eyes wide with terror as he struggled weakly against his restraints.

"Meet our friend here," Junior said, his tone almost cheerful. "He had a lot to say about loyalty—right before he sold us out to The Veil."

A murmur of shock rippled through the group, breaking the fragile silence. Tory's pulse quickened. This wasn't just a display of power—it was a declaration of war.

Junior's smile hardened as he raised his pistol again, aiming it at the captive's head. "Let this be a lesson," he said, his voice icy. "Loyalty isn't optional."

The gunshot was quick, brutal, and final. The captive crumpled to the ground, blood pooling beneath him.

Tory clenched her fists, her breath hitching. Junior's ruthlessness was nothing new, but seeing it up close was a grim reminder of the lengths he was willing to go to maintain control.

The lieutenants remained frozen, their faces carefully blank, but Tory could see the cracks forming. Subtle glances exchanged, shifting postures—signs of discontent that Junior either didn't notice or chose to ignore.

"Junior's losing them," she whispered to Antonio, her voice tight with unease.

Antonio nodded, his expression grim. "He's holding onto power by sheer force, but that won't last. Fear's a leash that snaps eventually."

Before Tory could respond, a sharp voice rang out from the far end of the warehouse.

"Enough!"

A tall man with graying hair and the unmistakable bearing of a military leader strode into the circle, flanked by half a dozen armed men. Dominic Crane. Tory recognized him instantly—an underboss with enough influence to challenge Junior directly.

Crane's cold gaze swept over the group before settling on Junior. "You're out of line, kid," he said bluntly.

Junior stiffened, his smirk faltering for the first time. "Crane. Didn't expect you to show up."

"I'm here because you're making a mess," Crane said, his voice sharp and unyielding. "You think you can run this syndicate with brute force? You're delusional."

The tension between them crackled like static, the lieutenants exchanging uneasy glances as the power struggle played out before them.

From their hiding spot, Tory and Antonio watched in silence.

"This is it," Antonio murmured. "The tipping point."

Tory's gaze flicked between Junior and Crane, her mind racing. "If this turns into a firefight, we're all screwed."

Junior stepped back, raising his hands in mock surrender. "Relax," he said, his smirk returning, though it lacked conviction. "No need to get blood on the merchandise."

Crane didn't look convinced, but he motioned for his men to stand down.

"This isn't over," Crane said coldly.

"It never is," Junior replied, his tone laced with mockery.

As Crane and his men departed, Junior turned back to the group. "Anyone else have something to say?"

The silence that followed was deafening.

# CHAPTER 5
# UNMASKING THE ENEMY

THE STORM that had grumbled on the horizon all evening finally unleashed its fury. Sheets of rain lashed the city, hammering the pavement and turning the streets into rivers of fractured neon. Tory Wayne pulled her hood tighter, her sharp green eyes scanning the rain-blurred skyline as she moved purposefully through the downpour. The steady rhythm of water against asphalt masked her footsteps, but not the unease prickling at the edges of her senses.

Ahead, the crumbling factory loomed—a hulking silhouette of decay on the city's fringes. Once a monument to industrial ambition, it was now just another skeleton of neglect, its sagging roof and shattered windows exhaling the cold breath of abandonment. But tonight, it wasn't empty. Tory knew the truth: the factory was a hub of activity, its purpose hidden beneath layers of The Veil's careful obfuscation.

Her contact's words rattled in her mind: "Whatever they're moving, it's not just another shipment. It'll change the game—for good."

Tory adjusted her hood, stepping lightly as she approached the perimeter. Her breath fogged the air, mixing with the faint chemical tang of ozone and industrial decay. A rusted chain-link fence surrounded the factory, its edges sagging under years of neglect. The only light came from a flickering bulb above the main entrance, where two guards stood. They were dressed in black, their casual postures belied by the restless way their hands hovered near their weapons.

She moved toward the building's rear, avoiding the splash of puddles as her eyes darted to the shadows. The rain cloaked her approach, but she'd learned long ago not to rely on the elements. The Veil didn't leave anything to chance. If they wanted this shipment hidden, the defenses would be layered and deliberate.

At the loading dock, Tory found what she was looking for: an open window just large enough to slip through. Her fingers curled around the wet metal frame as she pulled herself up, her boots finding purchase on the slippery surface. She crouched for a moment, listening. The steady drum of rain against the roof muffled all but the faintest murmurs of activity inside.

The air was colder here, the factory walls trapping dampness and the faint stench of oil. Tory slipped inside, her movements silent, landing lightly on the cement floor. The shadows swallowed her, her figure blending into the maze of rusted machinery and conveyor belts.

The factory's interior was no less foreboding than its exterior. Dust hung thick in the air, coating the abandoned rows of assembly lines and tools. The once-bright paint on the walls was faded and peeling, revealing the rusted metal beneath. But there was something else—a faint acrid odor, sharp and unfamiliar. Tory's instincts flared, a prickling unease settling in her chest.

This wasn't just another shipment. The Veil was building something here, something layered in secrecy and menace.

Ahead, the glow of a work lamp illuminated a cluster of crates, their surfaces marked with a cryptic insignia. Tory crept closer, her pistol drawn, every muscle in her body coiled with tension.

And then she saw him.

Detective Lucas Harrison.

The sight froze her mid-step. He stood by the crates, his posture tense, his hand resting on the butt of his sidearm. Harrison wasn't just a relic of her past—he was one of the few people she'd trusted after her fall. But here he was, standing guard over The Veil's operation like a willing pawn.

"Harrison," she whispered, the name slipping out before she could stop herself.

His head snapped up, his hand instinctively gripping his weapon as his eyes searched the shadows. When his gaze landed on her, recognition flickered, followed by a jarring mix of relief and alarm.

"Tory?" he murmured, his voice barely audible over the pounding rain.

Neither of them moved for a moment, the tension between them thick enough to strangle.

"What the hell are you doing here?" Harrison finally asked, his voice low, edged with something she couldn't quite name.

Tory stepped closer, her pistol still aimed. "Funny, I was about to ask you the same thing."

Harrison's jaw tightened, his expression hardening. "It's not what you think."

"Really?" she shot back, her tone sharp. "Because it looks like you're babysitting a shipment for The Veil."

His lips pressed into a grim line. "You don't understand, Tory. This isn't a choice. It's survival."

Her laugh was bitter, cutting through the thick air. "Survival? That's your excuse? Selling out to them?"

"Call it what you want," he said sharply. "But they've got their hooks in everything—cops, politicians, courts. You don't fight something like that head-on. You play along, get close enough to see the cracks. That's the only way you can survive long enough to do anything about it."

Tory's grip tightened on her pistol. "So that's it? You've got some noble mission to take them down from the inside? Spare me, Harrison."

His voice dropped, low and raw. "I'm not asking for your trust, Tory. I'm asking you to be smart. If you blow this, they'll know, and we'll both be dead before morning."

Before she could respond, voices echoed through the factory. Both of them stiffened, their gazes snapping toward the source of the sound.

A group of men emerged from the shadows, their footsteps purposeful. At the center was Junior Davos, flanked by two lieutenants. But Tory's attention was drawn to the man walking beside them—a tall, impeccably dressed figure whose calm authority radiated like a storm's eye.

"Markham," Harrison muttered, his voice tight with unease.

Tory's stomach sank. She didn't need the name to know what he represented. This man wasn't just another cog in The Veil's machine—he was the hand turning the gears.

Junior's swagger seemed forced as he glanced at Markham, his usual bravado dimmed by the other man's presence. "Everything's ready to move, right?" Junior asked, his voice betraying a hint of nervousness.

Markham's smile was thin, his tone smooth and icy. "The shipment is proceeding as planned, Mr. Davos. But let's be clear—this isn't your operation. You're a facilitator, not a leader. Don't overstep."

Junior's smirk faltered, but he recovered quickly. "Of course. Just wanted to make sure we're on the same page."

Markham's gaze swept the room, pausing for a moment in the shadows where Tory and Harrison hid. Tory held her breath, every muscle locked in place. After what felt like an eternity, Markham turned back to Junior.

"This shipment is critical to our goals," Markham continued. "If anything goes wrong, you'll answer directly to me—and trust me, you won't enjoy that conversation."

Junior nodded stiffly, the tension in his frame betraying his fear.

Tory leaned closer to Harrison, her voice a whisper. "What's in the crates?"

Harrison's expression was grim. "Weapons. Tech. Maybe worse. They're arming for something big—something the city isn't ready for."

Tory's mind raced. The Veil wasn't just flexing their influence. They were preparing for war.

Before they could act, a loud crash echoed through the factory. One of the crates toppled, its contents spilling onto the floor.

The room erupted into chaos.

# CHAPTER 6
# THE TURNING POINT

THE CITY WAS UNRAVELING, its seams splitting under the weight of Junior Davos's ambition. Chaos seeped into every street corner, every shadowed alley, transforming San Francisco into a fractured warzone. Trust had crumbled, alliances were shattered, and Junior's all-out assault on the old syndicate order turned the streets into battlegrounds.

Fires burned in the gutters, throwing eerie shadows onto crumbling facades. Gunfire echoed through the alleys, sharp and relentless, while shouts of defiance clashed with the mournful howl of sirens. Smoke mingled with the tang of burning oil, the acrid stench clinging to everything.

Above it all, Tory Wayne stood on the rooftop of a dilapidated apartment building, the wind whipping at her jacket. Her sharp green eyes scanned the chaos below, taking in the burning cars and shattered storefronts that marked yet another skirmish in Junior's campaign for dominance.

Beside her, Antonio Alvarez leaned against the rooftop's ledge, the glow of his cigarette briefly illuminating his face. His usual smirk was nowhere to be found; instead, a grim determination settled into his features.

"You ever think about walking away?" Antonio asked, his voice low as he exhaled a plume of smoke into the night.

Tory's gaze didn't waver from the street below. "Walk away? From this city? From The Veil?"

"From everything," Antonio clarified, his tone uncharacteristically soft. "There's only so many fires you can fight before one of them burns you alive."

She hated how his words lingered in the air, the truth in them like a needle pressing against her ribs. "If you're looking for an exit, Antonio, you've got the wrong partner."

His smirk returned, faint and tinged with weariness. "Who said I'm looking for an exit? Maybe I'm just wondering how much fight you've got left."

"Enough," Tory snapped, her voice sharp as steel. She gestured toward the chaos below. "Look at him. He's not holding back anymore. Junior's cutting out the old guard, consolidating power, and The Veil must've promised him something big to make this worth the risk."

Antonio took another drag from his cigarette, his gaze following hers. "Or maybe they're just using him as a distraction. Let the city rip itself apart while they move their real pieces into place."

The thought made Tory's stomach churn, her jaw tightening. "Then we can't let him win. If Junior consolidates power, The Veil will have a puppet with unchecked influence. And that's something this city won't survive."

Antonio's sidelong glance was skeptical. "And what's your grand plan, Wayne? March into Junior's mansion, flash that green-eyed glare of yours, and tell him to play nice?"

Tory didn't answer right away. The truth was, she didn't have a clean answer. Weeks of chasing Junior, dismantling his operations piece by piece, had drained her reserves. But this wasn't just about stopping him—it was about uprooting The Veil before their tendrils dug too deep to sever.

Finally, she said, "We need leverage. Something to cut Junior off at the knees—and make The Veil think twice about using him again."

Antonio arched an eyebrow, suspicion flickering across his face. "Leverage like what?"

Tory reached into her jacket and pulled out a crumpled piece of paper, handing it to him.

Antonio unfolded it slowly, his eyes scanning the list of names and locations. "Blackwell?" he asked, though the answer was clear in her expression.

"Dirty cops, syndicate lieutenants, and even a few of Junior's inner circle," Tory said, her tone steely. "They're the glue holding him together. Take them out, and his empire collapses."

Antonio's expression darkened. "That's not leverage, Wayne. That's a damn hit list."

"Call it what you want," Tory replied, crossing her arms. "But if we destabilize him enough, The Veil will cut him loose. Once he's isolated, we take him down."

Antonio studied her, his fingers tapping the paper as he thought. "You've got guts. I'll give you that. But this plan of yours? It's suicide."

Tory turned to face him fully, her gaze unwavering. "I don't need your approval. Just your help."

A long silence stretched between them, the sound of distant gunfire filling the void. Finally, Antonio sighed, folding the paper and slipping it into his pocket. "Fine. But if this goes south, don't expect me to pull your ass out of the fire."

---

THE FIRST TARGET was a shipping depot in the industrial district—a critical hub for Junior's operations. Tory and Antonio approached under cover of darkness, the shadows wrapping around them like armor as they slipped past the chain-link fence.

The depot was heavily guarded, its perimeter lined with razor wire and patrolled by armed sentries. Floodlights cut through the dark, casting long, stark shadows across the asphalt.

Tory crouched low behind a stack of crates, her sharp eyes tracking the rhythmic movements of the guards. "This isn't Junior's style," she murmured.

Antonio nodded beside her. "No, this is The Veil. Junior doesn't have the discipline to run a setup this tight. They're pulling his strings harder than we thought."

The thought only sharpened Tory's resolve. If The Veil was this invested, whatever they were guarding wasn't just about Junior's ambitions—it was about their endgame.

"This is going to be loud," Antonio whispered, a faint smirk creeping back onto his face.

"That's the point," Tory replied, pulling a small, hand-built explosive from her jacket.

Antonio's eyebrows shot up. "Since when do you carry around bombs?"

"Since I stopped playing fair," she said, pressing the device against the lock on the main gate.

The explosion was sharp and bright, cutting through the stillness of the night like a gunshot. Shouts erupted from the guards as they scrambled toward the breach, their weapons drawn.

Tory and Antonio moved swiftly, slipping through the chaos and into the depot's maze of shipping containers. The air inside was thick with the smell of oil and damp metal, every step echoing faintly against the corrugated steel walls.

Near the center of the depot, they found the shipment: rows of heavy-duty crates, each one stamped with the same cryptic insignia Tory had seen at the factory.

Antonio pried one of the crates open, revealing rows of sleek, black weapons—military-grade, lethal, and gleaming in the dim light.

"Junior's arming for a war," Antonio muttered, his tone grim.

Tory's stomach twisted. This wasn't just about syndicate politics anymore. Junior was stockpiling for something far more dangerous.

"We can't let this leave the city," she said.

Antonio nodded. "Agreed. But unless you've got a plan to blow this place sky-high without drawing the whole damn syndicate down on us..."

Tory's mind raced. There was no way to destroy the shipment quietly, but they couldn't leave it intact. Finally, she pulled out her phone and dialed a number.

WHEN THE EXPLOSION tore through the depot fifteen minutes later, the flames painted the night sky with streaks of orange and black. Tory and Antonio stood at the edge of the industrial district, the acrid stench of burning metal clawing at their throats.

"That'll get their attention," Antonio said, lowering a pair of binoculars.

"Good," Tory replied, though her stomach churned. The depot was gone, but the fire had only just begun.

Antonio glanced at her. "What's next?"

Tory's jaw tightened as she stared into the blaze. "We go to Junior. If we don't stop him now, there won't be anything left to save."

Antonio chuckled darkly, flicking his cigarette to the ground. "Straight into the lion's den. You've got a death wish, Wayne."

She turned to face him, her green eyes blazing with determination. "No. I've got a plan. And if Junior wants a war, we're going to give him one."

# CHAPTER 7
# TRUTHS REVEALED

THE WAREHOUSE WAS a cavern of shadows, its silence thick and oppressive. Rusted beams groaned faintly above, the sound amplified in the still air. The sharp tang of oil and gunpowder clung to the walls, lingering like a warning. A single bulb swung gently from its cord, casting fractured light across the crates and machinery. Each flicker threw jagged shadows that seemed to breathe with the shifting light.

Tory Wayne stood near the center of it all, her pistol a cold, familiar weight in her hand. Her knuckles whitened as she tightened her grip, the tension coiling in her chest like a spring ready to snap. This wasn't just another confrontation—this was the moment everything would either shatter or fall into place.

Across the room stood Junior Davos, flanked by two armed enforcers. His smirk was as sharp as ever, but the tension in his jaw betrayed him. Behind him, almost obscured by shadows, loomed Markham, The Veil's liaison.

Markham's calculating eyes swept the room, pausing briefly on each figure before settling on Junior. He adjusted the cuffs of his suit with slow, deliberate precision, exuding the calm authority of someone who thrived in chaos.

"You've done well, Junior," Markham said, his voice smooth, each word measured. "But let's not mistake initiative for leadership. Remember why you're here."

Junior bristled, his smirk faltering for a split second before he recovered. "I don't need a reminder," he snapped, his tone sharper than intended.

Markham raised an eyebrow, his expression unchanging. "Good. Because mistakes at this stage aren't just costly—they're fatal."

The words hung in the air, heavy with finality. Junior's smirk returned, but it was brittle, his bravado struggling to mask the unease that settled around him like a noose.

"You've been busy, Wayne," Junior called out suddenly, his voice cutting through the silence like a blade. He leaned against a crate, his smirk hardening. "Supply lines torched. Lieutenants jumping ship. You've made quite the mess."

Tory stepped out of the shadows, her sharp green eyes locking onto him. Her steps were deliberate, her expression cold. "Somebody had to clean up after you, Junior. Might as well be me."

His laugh was harsh, echoing in the cavernous space. "You think you're cleaning up? All you've done is piss off the wrong people. Do you really think this ends with me?"

Tory's gaze shifted to Markham, who watched the exchange with the faintest hint of amusement. "No," she said, her voice cutting through the room like ice. "But it starts with you."

Junior's smirk widened, his arrogance sharpening. "You think this is about me? I'm just the beginning. The Veil is inevitable. You're fighting a war you've already lost."

Markham stepped forward, his polished shoes clicking softly against the concrete. His presence filled the room like a storm gathering strength. "Ah, Ms. Wayne. Still clinging to that quaint notion of salvation." His faint smile sent a chill through her. "Tell me, does it keep you warm at night?"

Tory raised her pistol, her gaze unwavering. "And what's your idea of salvation, Markham? Turning the city into your personal chessboard?"

His smile widened slightly, though it didn't reach his eyes. "Not a chessboard. A machine. Efficient. Profitable. Controlled." His tone was maddeningly calm, as though explaining an undeniable truth. "The city is broken, Ms. Wayne. We're not destroying it—we're perfecting it. Refining the process."

Tory's stomach churned. "You're not refining anything. You're just another group of criminals grabbing for more power."

Markham's chuckle was soft, dismissive. "Power is a tool, Ms. Wayne. Chaos, on the other hand... chaos is bad for business. People like Junior are useful precisely because they create chaos—chaos we then neutralize. It's a service, really."

Tory's grip on her pistol tightened, her pulse hammering in her ears. "And what about the people caught in between? What happens to them?"

Markham's gaze didn't waver. "They adapt. Or they become irrelevant. Progress demands sacrifice." He tilted his head slightly, his tone almost condescending. "You, of all people, should understand that."

The weight of his words pressed down on her, each syllable a bitter reminder of the compromises she'd made.

"This ends tonight," Tory said, her voice steady despite the storm raging inside her. "I don't care how deep your roots go or how many people you've bought. You're not taking this city."

Junior laughed then, sharp and bitter. "Bold words for someone out of options."

Tory smirked, a flicker of defiance lighting her eyes. "Who says I'm out of options?"


THE FIRST SHOT shattered the tension, the crack of the muzzle echoing through the warehouse. Tory dove behind a stack of crates as chaos erupted around her.

Gunfire tore through the air, bullets ricocheting off metal beams and machinery. Shadows shifted with every flash of light, figures darting between cover as shouts filled the space.

Tory caught a glimpse of Antonio returning fire, his expression grim as he fired from behind a stack of pallets. The sharp smell of gunpowder mixed with the acrid tang of fear, the cacophony of violence swallowing every thought.

"Junior's freelancers!" Antonio shouted, his voice cutting through the chaos.

Tory's heart pounded as she peeked out from behind the crate, her gaze locking onto Junior, who crouched behind cover, barking orders to his men. Markham, however, had vanished into the shadows.

"Antonio!" Tory shouted, her voice strained. A sharp cry cut through the air, and her blood ran cold.

She turned, scanning the room frantically. "Antonio!"

No response.

Her breath caught as she spotted a figure slumped against a crate, a pool of blood spreading beneath him. She moved cautiously, her grip on her pistol tightening as she approached. Relief washed over her when she realized it wasn't Antonio—but it was fleeting.

Where is he?

WHEN THE DUST SETTLED, the silence was deafening. Tory stood amidst the wreckage, her pistol raised as she scanned the room.

Junior sat slumped against a wall, his shoulder soaked with blood from a gunshot wound. His smirk was gone, replaced by a grimace of pain and rage.

"You don't get it," he snarled, his voice hoarse. "Even if you kill me, The Veil will replace me. You can't win."

"Maybe not," Tory said, her tone cold. "But I can make it harder for them."

She raised her pistol, her finger tightening on the trigger.

"Tory, wait!"

Antonio's voice rang out, sharp and commanding.

Her gaze snapped to him, her grip on the weapon faltering. Antonio stepped forward, his hands raised.

"We need him alive," he said. "He's our only link to The Veil's higher-ups. If we kill him, we lose everything."

Tory hesitated, her breath coming in short bursts as she weighed his words. Finally, she lowered her weapon, her jaw tightening.

"You're lucky," she muttered to Junior.

Junior's laugh was low and bitter. "No, you're the one who's screwed. The Veil knows everything about you, Wayne. Your past. Your failures. Your weaknesses. You think they'll let you walk away from this?"

Later, as the rain came down in sheets outside the warehouse, Tory stared at her phone, Elliot Moore's warning ringing in her ears:

*"You're not just an obstacle, Tory. You're part of their plan."*

The message she received next was worse:

**"We've been watching you. Every step. Every failure. Every secret. You're next."**

Tory's breath caught as the realization settled like lead in her chest. She wasn't just hunting The Veil—they'd been hunting her all along.

Lightning flashed across the city, illuminating the shattered skyline. As Tory slid her phone into her pocket, her resolve hardened.

If The Veil thought they could control her, they were about to learn just how wrong they were.

The war wasn't over. It was only beginning.

The End

# MARKED

## A SHORT THRILLER

# UNTITLED

**Prologue: Shadows Tighten**

The storm had rolled in just after sundown, blanketing the city in a curtain of rain and shadows. From her perch on the crumbling rooftop of a derelict warehouse, Tory Wayne watched the streets below, her sharp green eyes scanning the pools of light cast by flickering streetlamps. The rain soaked through her jacket, dripping off the strands of her damp hair, but she stayed motionless, her pistol a familiar weight in her hand.

Somewhere in the distance, a siren wailed, its mournful cry swallowed by the constant drum of water on asphalt. Below, a black sedan idled at the curb, its tinted windows glinting ominously. She recognised the vehicle—it had been following her for days, its silent presence more threatening than a gunshot.

Tory's pulse quickened. This was no coincidence.

The Veil was done watching from the shadows.

Her breath misted in the cold air as she raised a pair of binoculars to her eyes. Through the rain-speckled glass, she caught a glimpse of movement inside the car. A shadow leaned forward—a figure in a suit, their silhouette sharp against the muted glow of the dashboard.

A sharp jolt of recognition hit her. The man was Markham, The

Veil's ice-cold enforcer. He wasn't just here for surveillance. This was an escalation.

She adjusted her grip on the pistol. The warehouse behind her was empty now, just another relic of a city that had moved on without it. But tonight, it was her battleground. If The Veil wanted her, they'd have to come and take her.

A flicker of movement in the corner of her vision snapped her focus to the adjacent alley. Two figures slipped through the shadows, their black coats blending seamlessly into the night. She recognised the fluid precision of their movements—professional, methodical. The kind of operatives The Veil deployed when words failed and violence became necessary.

Tory crouched, her muscles coiling with readiness.

Her earpiece crackled to life. "Wayne," a familiar voice whispered. It was Hank Waite, her former partner and one of the few people she trusted. "You've got company. Two at your six, and a third circling from the east."

"I see them," Tory murmured, her voice steady. "What about the car?"

"Driver's still inside. Markham's not moving yet." A pause, filled with static and tension. "They're here to test you, Tory. See how far you'll run before they tighten the noose."

"I'm not running," she said.

She took a slow breath, steadying her aim as the first operative moved into the open. The man was tall, his face obscured by the low brim of his cap. He advanced cautiously, his footsteps silent on the wet pavement.

Tory waited until he was close enough to see the faint glint of a weapon in his hand. Then, with surgical precision, she fired.

The crack of her pistol shattered the night, the shot striking true. The man crumpled to the ground, his weapon clattering uselessly beside him.

The others reacted instantly, their movements fluid as they sought cover. A second shot rang out, narrowly missing Tory's shoulder as she ducked behind a rusted ventilation unit.

"Wayne, you need to move!" Hank's voice was sharper now, tinged with urgency. "This isn't just about the operatives. They've got Markham here for a reason."

"I know," she snapped, her mind racing.

She peeked out from behind her cover, her sharp eyes catching the second operative's shadow against the rain-slick brick wall. He was flanking her, trying to close the distance.

Her fingers tightened around the pistol, her breath slowing as she took aim.

Then she saw it. A red dot, faint but unmistakable, dancing across her chest.

"Sniper," she whispered, ducking instinctively as the crack of a distant rifle split the air. The bullet struck where she'd been a moment before, sending shards of brick scattering across the rooftop.

"Tory!" Hank's voice was frantic now. "They're boxing you in. You've got to—"

The line went dead, replaced by a high-pitched whine of interference.

Tory's mind raced as she calculated her next move. Staying put was suicide, but the sniper had the advantage, and Markham was still waiting below. This wasn't just a hunt—it was a message.

She glanced at the edge of the rooftop, her pulse hammering in her ears. The gap between this building and the next was wide, but it was her only chance.

Gathering her strength, she bolted toward the ledge, her boots pounding against the slick surface. The sniper's rifle cracked again, the bullet skimming so close she felt its heat against her arm.

With a final burst of speed, she leapt into the void.

Time seemed to stretch as the wind tore at her clothes, the city below a blur of rain and light. She hit the opposite rooftop with a grunt, rolling to absorb the impact as her shoulder slammed against the rough surface. Pain lanced through her, but she pushed herself up, adrenaline drowning out the ache.

She didn't stop to look back.

Far below, Markham watched her silhouette vanish into the night. His expression was impassive as he reached for his phone, dialing a number with practiced ease.

"She's resourceful," he said into the receiver, his tone calm but cold. "But predictable. The Broker will want to know."

A pause, then a faint smile curved his lips. "No. She won't escape for long. This is exactly where we want her."

As the call ended, Markham leaned back in his seat, his gaze fixed on the rain-drenched city. Tory Wayne wasn't just a threat to neutralize. She was a pawn to move.

And the next move was already in play.

# CHAPTER 1
# THE VEIL UNVEILED

THE STREETS of Chinatown pulsed with late-night energy, the glowing red lanterns casting fractured shadows on the rain-slick pavement. Tory Wayne moved with practiced ease, her eyes scanning the crowd for faces that lingered too long, glances that held too much weight. The memory of the sniper's laser dot on her chest still coiled in her muscles, making her every movement sharp and deliberate. Here, in the noise and chaos of the city's underbelly, it was easy to disappear —or so she hoped.

Her destination wasn't far now, tucked away in a forgotten alley behind a dimly lit noodle shop. The burn in her shoulder flared with every step, a reminder of the sniper's near miss. The makeshift bandage she'd tied beneath her jacket was holding, but the memory of the shot still reverberated in her chest. Every instinct told her to go underground, to disappear until the heat dissipated. But if Markham and his men thought she'd back down, they didn't know her well enough. The rain stung her skin, mingling with the sweat slicking her neck, but she didn't slow. The hum of distant neon buzzed in time with the chatter of late-night vendors. The scents of the street shifted with each step—cloying incense from a vendor's stand, the sharp tang of freshly sliced ginger, and the faint metallic bite of rain-soaked pavement. The din of laughter and clinking dishes rolled out of open doorways, masking the subtle undertone of hurried whispers and fleeting glances. The acrid tang of soy and grease mingled with the occasional whiff of rain-soaked stone. Above, lanterns swayed, their dim light twisting the alley into something alive, watching, waiting. Tory slipped past a group of street performers, their erratic drumbeats echoing her quickening heartbeat. She adjusted the baseball cap shielding her face and kept her pace casual, blending in with the late-night foot traffic. But her pulse was anything but calm.

The sniper's rifle hadn't just grazed her arm; it had rattled something deeper. This wasn't just about survival anymore—it was about the fact that The Veil didn't see her as a threat to destroy. They saw her as a piece on their board, something to manipulate. And that was worse than any bullet.Every nerve screamed at her to turn back, but the stakes were too high. She didn't have the luxury of hesitation—not now, when every lead could be the difference between survival and obliteration. Still, she couldn't ignore the unease coiling in her chest, the faint but persistent voice whispering that she was walking straight into The Veil's clutches. The memory of Lambert's last words gnawed at her: "Keep digging, and you won't like what you find." Every lead came with a cost, and Tory couldn't help but wonder how much more she could afford to lose.

The tip had been anonymous, the kind that usually led to a trap. But if it was true—if The Veil really operated out of a hidden outpost here—then it was a risk she couldn't afford to ignore.

The deeper she went, the more the city's pulse seemed to fade. The distant din of vendors and laughter softened to a muffled hum, leaving only the rhythmic drip of rain and the shuffle of her boots. It was as though the alley existed outside the city, a place forgotten and waiting for shadows to claim it. Every sound—every dripping pipe, every faint shuffle—felt amplified, pressing against her ears. Her hand hovered near the compact pistol at her hip as she scanned the area. A shimmer near the ground caught her eye—something too clean, too deliberate to belong here. The stench of mildew and garbage made her nose crinkle, but it was the silence—the kind that felt too deliberate—that sent a shiver down her spine. A faint rustle made her pause, her hand instinctively brushing the compact pistol beneath her jacket. She scanned the darkness, but the only movement came from the swaying remnants of an old poster, its faded slogan long forgotten. With a steadying breath, she pressed on, her senses heightened.

She stepped into the shadows, her hand brushing the compact pistol holstered under her jacket.

---

No sign marked the outpost, no obvious entrance to betray its presence. Tory paused mid-step, her gaze catching a faint shimmer—an anomaly that didn't belong. She crouched by a puddle, its surface rippling faintly from the dripping rain, and there it was: a concealed doorway, visible only in the distorted reflection. Her pulse quickened as she straightened, the quiet hum of technology hidden within the decrepit surroundings confirming her suspicions.

"Gotcha," she muttered under her breath.

Tory crouched, inspecting the edge of the door. A sleek keypad glowed faintly beside it, its design incongruous with the otherwise decrepit surroundings. This wasn't just some hideout; it was a fortified operation.

Pulling a slim device from her pocket, she connected it to the keypad. The tiny screen flickered to life as the device ran through a sequence of codes. Seconds ticked by, each one stretching longer than the last.

"Come on," Tory whispered, glancing over her shoulder.

The device beeped softly, and the door clicked open. She slipped inside, the darkness swallowing her whole.

---

The interior was a stark contrast to the crumbling exterior. Polished floors gleamed under recessed lighting, and the air was chilled and sterile. Rows of servers hummed against one wall, their LED indicators blinking like fireflies. Shelves lined the space, filled with boxes labeled in a dozen different languages.

Tory moved cautiously, her steps silent as she scanned the room. A bulletin board on the far wall caught her attention, pinned with photographs, maps, and handwritten notes.

Her stomach tightened as she recognized one of the photos: herself, walking through a crowded street weeks earlier. The detail was surgical—notations of her every movement, the times she left her apartment, the routes she preferred when she thought no one was watching. It wasn't just data; it was her life, dissected and reduced to cold numbers. The familiar ache of vulnerability crept up her spine, but she forced it back. Vulnerability didn't survive in rooms like this.

Pinned beneath her photo was a note in block letters: *"Observe. Intercept."* Tory's mouth went dry. Her fingers brushed over the edge of another document, her stomach flipping as she scanned lines of surveillance reports. The details were painfully precise—times, locations, even a notation about the coffee shop she visited every Thursday. Her breath hitched as the scope of it hit her: she wasn't just being watched; she was being tracked.

"They've been watching me," she muttered, her voice barely audible.

Beside her photo was another, this one far older. It showed a man in a suit shaking hands with a smiling politician. Tory recognized the politician immediately—Mayor Conrad Ellison, one of San Francisco's most untouchable figures.

Ellison was in The Veil's pocket.

The implications hit her like a freight train. This wasn't just about the syndicate or the city's underworld. The Veil's reach extended into the halls of power, and if Ellison was compromised, so was half the city's infrastructure.

---

Tory's thoughts were interrupted by the sound of a door opening behind her. She spun, her pistol raised, as Jean Lambert stepped into the room.

Jean's sharp features twisted into a smirk, cold and calculated. "Still scurrying through shadows, Wayne? You've got a knack for being where you don't belong."

"Jean," Tory said, her voice cold. "Should've figured you'd be here."

Jean didn't flinch, her hands loose at her sides, but her stance carried the confidence of someone who'd already won. 'You're out of your depth, Wayne,' she said, her voice silk over steel. 'Turn around now, and I might just let you live

Tory's grip tightened on her pistol. "Funny. I was about to say the same thing." Jean tilted her head, her smirk widening into something sharper, predatory. Her fingers flexed at her sides, the subtle shift of her weight telegraphing the strike she was about to make. Tory's gaze flicked to Jean's hands, her grip on the pistol tightening as adrenaline coursed through her veins.

Jean's smirk widened, but there was no humor in it. "You have no idea what you're dealing with. The Veil isn't some two-bit syndicate. It's the spine of this city. You cut us out, and all you'll have left is a broken mess—and no one to clean it up."

Tory's jaw clenched. "Save the sermon. I'm not here for philosophy."

Jean's eyes flicked toward the servers. "You really think you can dismantle us with a couple of stolen files? Go ahead. See how far that gets you."

Tory didn't hesitate. She fired a warning shot, the bullet grazing the wall inches from Jean's head.

Jean's smirk disappeared, replaced by a glare. "Big mistake."

———

THE ROOM ERUPTED into chaos as Jean lunged, a blade flashing in her hand. Tory sidestepped, her pistol swinging down to block the strike. The impact jarred her arm, but she used the momentum to drive her knee into Jean's side.

Jean staggered but recovered quickly, slashing again. Tory ducked, the blade slicing through the air above her head. She retaliated with a sharp punch to Jean's jaw, sending the other woman sprawling into a shelf.

Jean snarled, grabbing a heavy metal case and swinging it toward

Tory. Tory barely raised her arm in time, the edge of the case glancing off her forearm before slamming into her ribs. She staggered, the impact stealing her breath as her back hit the wall. Pain radiated from her shoulder down to her elbow, but she gritted her teeth and pushed off, dodging Jean's next swing by a hair's breadth. The crash of the case hitting the floor echoed like a gunshot, and Tory seized the opening, driving her knee into Jean's midsection. The force sent Tory stumbling back, her shoulder slamming into the wall. Pain shot through her arm, but she didn't let it slow her down.

With a desperate lunge, she swept Jean's legs out from under her, sending her crashing to the floor. Tory pinned her with a knee to the chest, her pistol aimed squarely at Jean's face.

"Where's Markham?" Tory demanded, her voice ice.

Jean gritted her teeth, blood trickling from the corner of her mouth. "You're out of your depth, Wayne. Markham's just a cog in the machine. You'll never reach The Broker."

The words sent a chill down Tory's spine, but she didn't let it show. "I guess I'll just have to start with you."

Jean's smirk returned, faint but defiant. "Do it, then. See how long you survive after."

Her hand trembled, just slightly, as Jean's words gnawed at her resolve. She wanted to believe she could cut through The Veil's web with force, but the scope of it—it was too big, too insidious. Was she just another player in a game she barely understood?

Jean's laugh was low and mocking. "Time's up."

---

TORY SWORE UNDER HER BREATH, grabbing a nearby USB drive and jamming it into the nearest server. The progress bar moved agonisingly slowly, each percentage ticking upward as though mocking her. Her ears strained against the humming servers, the faint sound of approaching boots sending adrenaline coursing through her veins. She counted the steps—three sets, no, four. The hallway wasn't wide enough for them all to enter at once. Good. She could use that. The files downloaded at a crawl as the sound of footsteps echoed in the hallway.

The drive ejected just as the first gunshots rang out, bullets tearing into the room. Every piece of intel she'd ever gathered felt like a lifeline slipping through her fingers. This time, it wasn't just about exposing corruption—it was about staying ahead of something she couldn't yet see. The weight of the USB in her pocket was a promise and a threat all at once. Tory dove for cover, returning fire as she made her way to the exit.

She reached the door, her heart pounding, and glanced back. Jean was gone.

Outside, the rain had picked up, drenching her as she melted into the shadows. Tory's breath came in ragged bursts as she pressed herself against the damp brick wall, her pulse hammering in her ears. The USB drive in her pocket felt like a burning coal, its weight a constant reminder of what she'd uncovered—and the danger it brought. The Veil wasn't just watching her; they were closing in, and every second she stayed alive felt like a defiance against impossible odds.

Whatever was on it, one thing was clear: this was just the beginning.

Tory glanced over her shoulder, her sharp green eyes scanning the street.

She was no longer just hunting The Veil.

Now, they were hunting her.

# CHAPTER 2
# PLAYING BOTH SIDES

THE PENTHOUSE at the Grand Horizon exuded power, the kind of place where deals that shaped the city were sealed with a smile and a signature. Gleaming marble floors caught the faint glow of San Francisco's skyline, and the vast windows framed the city like a glittering prize waiting to be claimed. Tory Wayne stood at the edge of the room, her reflection faintly superimposed on the glass. The bruises from her escape still throbbed beneath her jacket, a reminder of just how high the stakes had become.

Behind her, Antonio Alvarez poured two fingers of scotch into a crystal tumbler. "You're quiet tonight," he said, his voice carrying an edge of curiosity.

Tory turned, her sharp green eyes narrowing. "I just broke into one of The Veil's outposts and barely made it out alive. Forgive me if I'm not in the mood for small talk."

Antonio raised his glass, his smirk faint. "Touché." Tory's hand twitched, wanting to snatch the glass from his hand and hurl it against the marble floor. The ease with which Antonio operated, the arrogance in his every move, grated against her nerves. She had come within inches of dying at that outpost, but to him, it seemed like just another calculated risk.

"You think this is a game," she said, her voice barely above a whisper. "But you're not the one they're hunting."

Tory crossed the room, her movements sharp and deliberate. "You knew what I'd walk into, didn't you?"

Antonio turned slightly, the crystal tumbler catching the dim light. "I don't know what you're talking about," he said, his smirk lazy but his eyes sharp.

"Don't play coy," Tory snapped, her voice low but cutting. "You sent me to that outpost blind, knowing full well The Veil would be watching."

Antonio's smirk didn't falter, but his eyes darkened slightly. "What makes you say that?"

"Because you always know," she said, her tone icy. "And because you didn't warn me."

Antonio sipped his drink, taking his time. "I didn't think you'd actually go. You have a habit of sticking your head into places it doesn't belong."

Tory's temper flared, but she forced herself to stay calm. "What's your angle, Antonio? Why are you still playing this game?"

He leaned against the bar, swirling the amber liquid in his glass. "Simple, Wayne. Survival. And I've learned the trick is making sure someone else takes the fall."

---

TORY DIDN'T TRUST ANTONIO. She hadn't for a long time. But she also couldn't afford to ignore him. He had a way of slipping into places she couldn't, of gathering intel she desperately needed.

"I found something," she said, pulling the USB drive from her jacket pocket. "Files from the outpost."

Antonio arched a brow. "And you're telling me this because...?"

"Because you have connections inside The Veil," she said bluntly. "Connections I don't."

Antonio chuckled softly. "You want me to dig through your stolen files? Risk my neck for whatever you pulled out of their servers?"

"Yes," Tory said.

His smile faded, replaced by something sharper. "And what's in it for me?"

Tory stepped closer, her voice low. "How about staying ahead of whatever The Veil is planning? Or are you fine waiting until they decide you're expendable?"

Antonio studied her for a long moment, then set his glass down with a faint clink. "Fine. I'll take a look."

---

WHILE ANTONIO WORKED on decrypting the files, Tory paced the room, her mind racing. The Veil wasn't just a syndicate—they were an empire, with tendrils that stretched far beyond San Francisco. The more she uncovered, the more it felt like she was standing on the edge of a precipice, staring into an abyss she couldn't fully comprehend.

"You're going to wear a hole in the floor," Antonio said without looking up from his laptop.

Tory ignored him. "Do you think Markham answers to someone higher up?"

Antonio's fingers paused briefly on the keyboard. "If you're asking whether there's a bigger player in The Veil, the answer is yes."

"And who is it?"

He glanced at her, his expression unreadable. "They call him The Broker. No one's ever seen him. Hell, I'm not even sure he exists." Tory's chest tightened at the name. It was nothing more than a word— simple, innocuous—but the way Antonio said it, low and edged with unease, made it feel like a brand pressed against her skin. The Broker. A name that carried weight without substance, a phantom pulling strings from the shadows. If even Antonio—who seemed to know everything—treated the idea of him with caution, what did that mean for her? The thought of going after someone she couldn't see or predict sent a chill crawling up her spine, but she forced herself to push it aside. Fear wasn't an option anymore.

"The Broker," she repeated, testing the weight of it. "You're telling me this shadow puppet runs The Veil, and you've never even heard his voice?"

Antonio's lips quirked into a faint smirk. "I don't ask questions that get me killed. Maybe you should try it sometime."

Tory's stomach tightened. The Broker. It wasn't much, but it was more than she'd had before.

Antonio turned the laptop toward her. "Take a look."

Tory leaned over the screen, scanning the decrypted files. They were a mix of surveillance logs, financial records, and coded messages. One document caught her attention: a list of names, including several high-ranking city officials and law enforcement officers.

"This is their network," Tory muttered. "Politicians, police, judges —they've bought them all."

Antonio nodded. "It's how they operate. Control the infrastructure, and you control the city."

Her gaze froze on one name: Mayor Conrad Ellison.

The letters seemed to burn into her vision, sharp and accusing. Ellison had been a cornerstone of San Francisco's politics for years, the kind of untouchable figure who gave speeches about integrity while shaking hands in back rooms. Seeing his name here wasn't just a revelation—it was a betrayal.

"Ellison's compromised," she said, her voice tight.

Antonio's smirk returned. "Welcome to the game, Tory. You didn't think it was just the criminals, did you?"

---

THEIR CONVERSATION WAS INTERRUPTED by a knock at the door.

Antonio frowned, his hand moving instinctively toward the pistol tucked under his jacket. "Expecting someone?"

Tory shook her head, her body tensing.

Antonio crossed the room and opened the door a crack. A man in a tailored suit stood on the other side, his expression calm but cold.

The man's gaze slid over Antonio like water, assessing him with the kind of detached precision that came from years of leverage and power. Dominic stepped forward, the air in the room shifting as his enforcers filed in behind him. They didn't reach for their weapons, but their presence was a silent threat.

"Nice place," Dominic remarked, his tone almost bored. His sharp eyes scanned the penthouse before landing on Tory. "Though I wasn't expecting company."

"Mr. Alvarez," the man said. "We need to talk."

Antonio opened the door wider, revealing two more men standing behind the first. Their presence radiated quiet menace, the kind that came from confidence backed by power.

"What brings The Veil to my doorstep?" Antonio asked, his voice casual.

The man stepped inside, his sharp eyes scanning the room. When his gaze landed on Tory, he paused, his lips curving into a faint smile.

"Well," he said, "this is unexpected."

Tory's hand twitched toward her pistol, but Antonio shot her a warning glance.

"This is Dominic," Antonio said. "One of The Veil's... accountants."

Dominic chuckled softly. "We prefer the term 'facilitators.'"

"Is this a social visit?" Antonio asked, his tone light.

Dominic's smile faded. "We have a problem. A certain outpost in Chinatown was breached last night. Files were stolen."

Tory kept her face neutral, her pulse hammering in her ears.

Dominic's gaze returned to her, his eyes narrowing slightly. "Do you know anything about that, Ms. Wayne?"

Tory tilted her head, her lips curving into a faint, defiant smile. "Why? Are you missing something important?"

Dominic's eyes narrowed slightly, his calm demeanour fraying at the edges. "You're bold for someone with so much to lose."

"Boldness is relative," Tory replied, her voice smooth. "Last I checked, having a drink wasn't a crime."

Dominic stepped closer, his voice lowering. "Old friends have a way of becoming liabilities. Be careful, Ms. Wayne. You're playing a game you can't win."

The tension in the room was suffocating. Tory forced herself to hold his gaze, her expression blank. "Should I?"

Dominic studied her for a moment, then turned back to Antonio. "We're cleaning up the mess. But if I find out you're involved..."

Antonio's smirk returned, faint and infuriating. "You'll be the first to know."

Dominic's eyes flicked between them once more before he turned and left, his enforcers trailing behind.

---

As THE DOOR CLOSED, Tory let out a breath she hadn't realized she was holding.

"You're playing a dangerous game," she said, her voice low. Tory studied Antonio as he leaned casually against the bar, his smirk in place as if none of this could touch him. But beneath the charm and swagger, she caught a flicker of something else—calculation, or maybe fear. Antonio was playing a game, all right, but for whom? The Veil? Himself? She wasn't sure if she admired his audacity or despised him for it.

Antonio chuckled, picking up his glass of scotch. "Aren't we all?"

Tory didn't respond. Her focus was on the USB drive and the names it contained.

Dominic's visit hadn't just confirmed her fears—it crystallised them. The Veil wasn't a shadow in the distance; it was here, surrounding her, its reach suffocating.

The Veil was everywhere.

And the only way to bring them down was to tear their network apart piece by piece.

# CHAPTER 3
# INTO THE DARKNESS

THE UNDERGROUND CLUB throbbed with quiet menace, its dim lighting a patchwork of flickering neon and deep shadows. The air was heavy with the tang of spilled liquor, sweat, and desperation, muffling the hum of whispered deals and low laughter. Private booths lined the walls like secrets waiting to be unearthed, their occupants shielded from prying eyes but never truly safe. The air was thick with smoke and the tang of spilled liquor, masking the sharper scent of desperation. Tory Wayne kept her head down as she navigated the crowd, her hood pulled low over her face.

Her pulse quickened with each step, every brush of a stranger's arm sparking her instincts. This wasn't just a den of criminals—it was a hunting ground. The Veil had eyes everywhere, and she couldn't shake the feeling that someone was already watching her, their gaze burning like a spotlight against her back.

Her contact had warned her about this meeting: the faction she was about to deal with wasn't interested in pleasantries or trust. But they had something she needed—access to The Veil's inner workings—and Tory wasn't about to let their reputation stop her.

She reached the booth tucked into the farthest corner of the club. Two men sat across from each other, their conversation interrupted as she approached. One was lean and sharp-eyed, his fingers drumming a restless beat on the table. The other was older, his expression carved into a mask of practiced indifference.

"You're late," the lean man snapped, his fingers drumming an erratic rhythm on the table. His sharp eyes flicked to her, sizing her up with a mixture of irritation and suspicion.

The older man's gaze lingered on her, cold and calculating, his silence heavy with judgment.

Tory slid into the booth without invitation, her eyes narrowing. "Traffic."

The older man studied her with cool detachment. "You're the one stirring up trouble for The Veil."

"Not trouble," Tory replied evenly. "Solutions. I heard you're looking for some."

---

THE OLDER MAN LEANED BACK, his fingers steepled. "You're bold to come here, Wayne. The Veil has eyes everywhere. If they catch you, you'll wish you were dead."

"I'll take my chances," Tory said. "You called me. Let's skip the part where you tell me how dangerous this is and get to why I'm here."

The lean man chuckled, but it was humorless. "She's got a mouth on her, doesn't she?"

The older man ignored him, his gaze never leaving Tory. "We're tired of Markham. His methods are reckless, and his ambitions threaten the balance we've worked to maintain. We want him out."

"And let me guess," Tory said, crossing her arms. "You want me to do it for you."

The older man's lips curved into a faint smile. "You have the skills, and you're already in his crosshairs. If you take him down, we'll give you access to The Veil's archives—everything you need to dismantle them."

Tory's stomach twisted. She didn't trust them, but their offer was tempting. She forced herself to weigh the risks against the rewards, but the scale tipped unevenly with every passing second. Taking down Markham would put her in the crosshairs of more than just The Veil. It would make her a target for their enemies too—the kind of people who dealt in silenced guns and shallow graves. But walking away wasn't an option either. The archives were a lifeline, dangling just out of reach, and she couldn't afford to let them slip through her fingers. The Veil's archives could expose their entire network, from their local operations to their global connections.

"And what happens after I do your dirty work?" Tory asked. "You just step in and take over?"

The lean man's grin widened. "That's none of your concern."

"Actually, it is," Tory said coldly. "I'm not trading one devil for another."

The older man's expression darkened. "You don't have the luxury of picking your devils, Ms. Wayne. Do this, or walk out of here with nothing." Tory's eyes flicked to the lean man's hand, resting too casually on the edge of the table. His fingers brushed against the hilt of a knife—not a threat, not yet, but a silent reminder. She leaned forward slightly, meeting the older man's gaze. His expression didn't shift, but she caught the faintest flicker of amusement. They were testing her, probing for weakness, and she refused to give them the satisfaction.

THE AIR between them crackled with tension. Tory leaned forward, her voice low. "Fine. I'll do it. But don't think for a second I won't burn you down too if you get in my way."

The older man nodded, his smile returning. "We'll be in touch."

Tory stood, her gaze lingering on the pair for a moment before she turned and disappeared into the crowd.

BACK OUTSIDE, the cool night air hit her like a slap. Tory's boots echoed against the slick pavement as she moved quickly, her breath visible in the chilled air. She kept her hand close to the knife tucked into her jacket, her senses still on high alert. The city's shadows felt alive, curling around her like silent predators. A faint shuffle behind her made her pulse quicken. She didn't turn, didn't break her stride, but her hand brushed the knife in her jacket pocket. The sound stopped, then started again—deliberate, measured, a hunter pacing its prey. She quickened her steps, scanning the street for an escape route, but the shadows closed in, thick and unyielding. Every sound—the distant roar of an engine, the faint crackle of a streetlamp—pricked at her nerves, each one a reminder of how thin the line was between hunter and prey. She walked quickly, her mind racing. Agreeing to their terms was a calculated risk, but she had no intention of following through. Markham was a threat, but so were they.

Her phone buzzed in her pocket. She pulled it out, her heart sinking when she saw the name on the screen: **Antonio.**

She answered, her voice tight. "What?"

"Charming as ever," Antonio drawled, his voice a mix of sarcasm and tension. "You know, most people check in after making deals with devils."

"Why?"

"Because I just heard an interesting rumor," Antonio said. "You've made a deal with a faction inside The Veil. Care to explain?"

Tory stopped walking, her chest tightening. "How do you know that?" Antonio's words always had a way of slicing through her defenses, needling at the parts of her she didn't want to examine too closely. She knew he was right—teaming up with the faction was reckless. But it was also the only move she could see.

"What's your play, Antonio?" she muttered, more to herself than to him. "You're not exactly on the moral high ground here."

"Let's just say I have friends in low places," Antonio replied, his voice tightening. "Friends who've seen what happens when someone makes a deal like yours. Tell me, Tory—what's the endgame here? Or are you just hoping you won't be their next loose end?"

Tory's grip on the phone tightened. "I don't owe you an explanation."

"No," Antonio said, his voice hardening. "But you owe yourself one. If you think for a second they won't turn on you the moment you're useful, you're not as smart as I thought."

"I can handle them," Tory snapped.

"Can you?" Antonio challenged. "Because from where I'm standing, you're playing right into their hands."

Tory hung up without responding, shoving the phone back into her pocket.

---

LATER THAT NIGHT, Tory sat in her small apartment, her laptop open in front of her. She replayed the meeting in her mind, every word, every gesture. She didn't trust the faction, and she didn't trust Antonio. Antonio's words echoed in her mind, needling at the edges of her resolve. He always had a way of being right, but that didn't make him trustworthy. He was a player in the same game, after all, moving pieces she couldn't see. And the faction? They were worse—wolves cloaked in civility, offering help with one hand while hiding a blade in the other.

But she trusted herself.She stared at the dim glow of her laptop screen, the decrypted files casting faint shadows across her cluttered desk. The faces and names staring back at her were more than just entries in The Veil's network—they were proof of how deep the corruption ran. But even with the data she had, the picture wasn't complete. She needed the archives to see the full scope of the game she was playing.

Her hand hovered over the USB drive for a moment before she pulled it free, her movements deliberate. This wasn't a choice—it was a necessity.

Her gaze fell on the USB drive still plugged into the laptop. The files she'd decrypted earlier had revealed pieces of The Veil's network, but they were incomplete. The archives promised by the faction could give her everything she needed to tear them apart.

But if Antonio was right—and he usually was—then working with them might lead her into a trap.

Tory leaned back in her chair, her jaw tight.

She'd already made her decision.

She didn't flinch from the darkness anymore; it had become her ally, her cover. If bringing The Veil down meant stepping deeper into its shadows, she'd do it without hesitation. The only question was whether she'd find the light again on the other side.

# CHAPTER 4
# JUNIOR'S GAMBIT

THE OLD FACTORY hummed with unease, its cavernous ceilings swallowing whispers and turning every creak of rusted metal into a gunshot. The air reeked of oil and damp concrete, thick with the ghosts of abandoned machinery. Shadows twisted across the floor, curling around crates stacked like monuments to a forgotten empire. Tory Wayne crouched behind a row of steel beams, her sharp green eyes locked on the group gathered in the center of the space.

Junior Davos stood at the heart of it all, his tailored suit a stark contrast to the hardened syndicate lieutenants surrounding him. Junior's smirk was painted on, but the restless twitch of his fingers against the table and the sharp flick of his eyes to his lieutenants told a different story. He was a man balancing on the edge of a blade, projecting strength while desperately clinging to control.

"This isn't a negotiation," Junior said, his voice sharp enough to cut through the factory's oppressive air. "I'm done waiting for Markham and his suits to figure out whose side they're on. From now on, we're doing things my way."

The lieutenants exchanged uneasy glances, their loyalty splintered. One of them, a wiry man with a scar running across his cheek, stepped forward.

"Junior," he said, his tone cautious, "you can't just cut out The Veil. They're the reason we're still standing."

Junior's smirk twisted into a sneer. "The reason we're still standing? Or the reason we're still crawling? Markham's got his hands so deep in our pockets, we might as well be working for him. That ends tonight."

---

TORY ADJUSTED HER POSITION, her pistol steady in her grip. Antonio Alvarez was crouched beside her, his expression unreadable as he watched the scene unfold.

"He's losing it," Antonio whispered.

"He's desperate," Tory replied. "And desperate men are dangerous."

Junior's voice rose, drawing their attention back to the group.

"I've already made my move," Junior announced, his smirk returning. "Markham thinks he's untouchable, but I've got eyes on him. When the time comes, we're going to remind The Veil who really runs this city."

The scarred lieutenant frowned. "And if they push back?"

Junior's smirk widened, his bravado swelling. "Then we push harder. Anyone who doesn't like it can join Markham in the ground."

The room erupted into murmurs, the lieutenants weighing their options. Tory felt the air shift—this wasn't just posturing anymore. Junior's plans were real, and the syndicate was on the edge of fracturing.

---

BEFORE TORY COULD PROCESS her next move, Junior turned abruptly, his sharp gaze sweeping the room.

"Speaking of eyes," he said, his voice dropping, "I know some of you are working against me. Feeding intel to The Veil. You think I don't see what's happening?"

The lieutenants froze, their expressions carefully neutral.

Junior's smirk faded, replaced by cold fury. "If you're not with me, you're against me. And I don't forgive traitors."

He snapped his fingers, and two of his men dragged a struggling figure into the circle. The man's face was battered, his hands bound.

"This," Junior said, gesturing to the captive, "is what happens to snitches."

Tory's chest tightened as Junior drew a knife from his jacket.

"Junior's going too far," she whispered to Antonio.

"And yet," Antonio replied, "he's doing exactly what The Veil would."

Tory's jaw clenched. She wanted to act, but she couldn't risk blowing her cover—not yet.

---

JUNIOR STEPPED CLOSER to the captive, his voice low and menacing. "I'll give the rest of you one chance. Swear your loyalty, or end up like him."

The lieutenants nodded, some slower than others, their silence brittle and uneasy. A few exchanged quick glances, the kind that spoke of doubt and simmering resentment, but none dared voice it. Not with Junior's bloody knife still glinting in the dim light.

Junior plunged the knife into the captive's chest without hesitation, the room erupting into shocked gasps. Tory's stomach twisted as the knife plunged into the captive's chest, the wet sound of steel tearing flesh reverberating in her mind. Her grip on her pistol tightened, her instincts screaming to act, to stop the carnage—but she didn't move. She couldn't. Every choice she'd made had brought her here, to this moment, and she wondered if the blood pooling on the floor would stain her hands too. She had made sacrifices before, but watching Junior turn violence into spectacle felt different—it felt like a line she was letting him draw in her name. She had learned to weigh desperation against opportunity, and this deal reeked of both. The Veil's archives were a prize she couldn't afford to ignore, but she could feel the noose tightening even as they spoke. These men weren't allies—

they were opportunists. And she had just walked into their trap willingly.

"Now," Junior said, wiping the blade clean on the captive's shirt, "let's talk about our next move."

---

THE MEETING DISSOLVED into tense conversations, Junior's men fanning out across the factory. Tory and Antonio used the chaos to slip deeper into the shadows, moving toward a side exit.

"That was a show of weakness," Antonio muttered, his tone clipped as they slipped deeper into the shadows.

Tory's jaw tightened. "Looked like a show of strength to me."

Antonio shot her a sidelong glance, his smirk tinged with disbelief. "You think killing one of his own makes him strong? That's fear, Tory. And fear doesn't lead—it burns everything down."

Tory exhaled sharply, the weight of his words settling like a stone in her chest. "Maybe. But fear also makes people dangerous. Junior's reckless, but that doesn't mean he's weak. It means we can use him."

Antonio shook his head. "He's losing control. The Veil's going to see this as a challenge, and they don't respond well to challenges."

Tory's mind raced. Junior's recklessness could destabilize the entire syndicate, but it could also create an opening to strike at Markham and The Veil.

"We can use this," Tory said, her voice steady. "Junior's making himself a target. If The Veil moves against him, we'll be ready."

"And if Junior moves first?" Antonio asked.

"Then we'll still be ready," Tory replied.

Antonio smirked faintly, his confidence returning. "You always make it sound so easy."

"It's not," Tory said. "But it's the only chance we've got."

---

THE DISTANT CLATTER of boots against concrete sent a jolt through Tory's nerves. She grabbed Antonio's arm, dragging him toward the exit. They slipped between the crates, the shadows offering thin cover as a flashlight beam swept over the space they'd just vacated. Her breath hitched, but she pressed on, her heart pounding with each step. The footsteps grew louder, more purposeful, and she quickened her pace, her heart pounding in time with their echoes. Just as they slipped through the door, a voice barked sharply behind them. Tory didn't turn to look—she didn't need to. The hunt was already beginning.They slipped out into the night, the cool air a stark contrast to the tension inside the factory.

As they moved through the shadows, Tory couldn't shake the feeling that they were walking a knife's edge. Junior's gambit had changed the game, and The Veil wouldn't let it go unanswered.

The city teetered on the edge of implosion, its balance crumbling with every fractured alliance and desperate move. Tory wasn't just caught in the fault line—she was part of it, her choices tearing loyalties apart and reshaping the game in ways she couldn't yet see.

# CHAPTER 5
# THE TIES THAT BIND

THE SAFE HOUSE sagged under the weight of neglect, its stained wallpaper curling away from the walls in damp, yellowed strips. Rain hammered against the boarded-up windows, each drop rattling like impatient fingers. The air was thick with the scent of mildew and rotting wood, and the faint wail of distant sirens seeped through the cracks, a reminder that danger was never far. Tory Wayne paced near the window, her sharp green eyes darting to the street below.

Antonio Alvarez sat at the splintering dining table, nursing a fresh cut across his cheekbone. His jacket was tossed over a chair, his shirt collar undone, but the cocky tilt of his smirk remained intact.

"You're going to wear a hole in the floor," Antonio said, dabbing at his cut with a damp cloth.

Tory ignored him, her gaze fixed on the alley outside. "Junior's men aren't going to give up, not after the stunt you pulled."

Antonio chuckled, though it lacked his usual warmth. "Stunt? I call it a tactical retreat."

Tory finally turned, her arms crossed. "Cornering Junior in his own backyard was tactical? Or were you just hoping to die with a little panache?"

Antonio leaned back in the rickety chair, wincing as it creaked beneath him. "I was gathering intel. Didn't expect him to be so... theatrical."

"Yeah, well, theatrics are Junior's specialty," Tory snapped. "You should've called me."

"I didn't need you to play backup," Antonio said, his smirk returning faintly. "But I'll admit, you've got decent timing."

Tory took a step closer, her frustration bubbling over. "You're reckless, Antonio. And now Junior's even more unstable. He's got a reason to come after both of us, and you're acting like this is a damn game."

Tory's pulse hammered as she spoke, her frustration tangled with something harder to name. Antonio always seemed to skate just above the chaos, his smirk intact even when the walls closed in. But this wasn't a game, and she couldn't afford to treat it like one—not when every move felt like stepping onto thin ice.

---

ANTONIO'S SMIRK faded as he stood, his gaze leveling with hers. "You think I don't know what's at stake? Junior's unraveling. He's a cornered animal, and cornered animals bite. But he's also useful—if we can control the chaos."

Tory scoffed. "Control Junior? He's already planning a coup against The Veil. He thinks if he takes out Markham, the syndicate will fall in line."

Antonio arched a brow. "You've been busy."

"I have contacts," Tory said flatly.

"And what's your plan?" Antonio asked. "Let him blow himself up and hope the fallout misses you?"

Tory's jaw tightened. "I'm going to use his desperation. If Junior's moving against Markham, it means The Veil's control is slipping. I can exploit that—cut the strings holding the syndicate together."

"Ambitious," Antonio said, his tone laced with sarcasm. "And how do you plan to deal with Junior after?"

Tory's silence was telling.

---

ANTONIO CROSSED THE ROOM, his footsteps deliberate. "You're too smart not to see what's happening here. You take out Markham, and Junior steps into the void. You leave Junior in play, and he'll tear the city apart trying to prove he's more than a puppet."

"I don't need a lecture," Tory said, her voice hard.

"Maybe you do," Antonio countered. "Because for all your planning, you're missing the bigger picture. This isn't about Junior or Markham—it's about The Veil. They don't lose. If one piece falls, they just replace it."

Tory met his gaze, her frustration giving way to something colder. "And what's your solution? Do nothing? Let them win?"

"No," Antonio said, his voice softening. "But you're not going to beat them by playing their game. Not without losing yourself in the process."

The words hit harder than she wanted to admit.

---

TORY TURNED AWAY, pacing back to the window. The rain was heavier now, streaking the glass with rivulets that blurred the city's outline.

"If you have a better idea, now's the time," she said.

Antonio hesitated, his expression unreadable. "Markham's not the top of the ladder," Antonio said, his voice lowering as if the walls themselves were listening. "There's someone above him. A name that comes up in whispers, even in the rooms where people aren't afraid of much. They call him The Broker."

Tory froze, the name slicing through her like a cold knife. The Broker. It wasn't just a name—it was a shadow looming over every piece of intel she'd uncovered, every thread she'd tried to unravel. Her fists clenched, the enormity of it pressing against her resolve. "And you waited until now to tell me?"

"I didn't know if it mattered," Antonio said. "The Broker isn't just pulling strings—he's weaving the whole web. Markham's just his messenger."

Tory turned, her fists clenched. "So you're saying Markham's nothing more than a distraction?"

"I'm saying that if you take him out, you'd better be ready for what comes next," Antonio said.

---

THE TENSION in the room was suffocating. Tory stared at Antonio, her mind racing. For all his flaws, he had a way of finding the cracks in her armor, of forcing her to confront truths she didn't want to see.

"You keep playing all sides," she said finally. "Junior, The Veil, me. What's your angle?"

Antonio shrugged, his smirk faint but present. "Survival. Same as you."

Tory stepped closer, her voice dropping. "If I find out you're lying to me—"

"You won't," Antonio interrupted, his tone steady. "Because if I was, I wouldn't be here."

The truth of that settled uncomfortably between them. Tory hated how much sense it made.

---

A SUDDEN NOISE outside snapped them both into action. Antonio grabbed his pistol, moving toward the door while Tory positioned herself at the window. A black sedan idled at the curb, its tinted windows obscuring whoever was inside.

"Junior's people?" Antonio asked.

Tory shook her head. "No. Too clean. That's The Veil."

Antonio let out a low whistle. "Guess they heard about your plan."

Tory's grip on her weapon tightened. "Guess so."

Antonio moved back to her side, his smirk returning despite the tension. "You're lucky I'm here," Antonio said, his smirk cutting through the tension like a blade.

Tory shot him a sidelong glance. "Lucky's not the word I'd use."

---

THE SEDAN IDLED, its engine a low, menacing growl that seemed to vibrate through the walls. Tory's breath slowed, her grip on her weapon tightening as the rain smeared the view through the cracked window. She could almost feel the weight of their gaze, heavy and calculating, as if they were deciding whether to strike now or let the tension fester. Tory tightened her grip on her weapon, her breath steady despite the spike of adrenaline. She could feel their eyes behind the tinted glass, waiting, weighing their next move. Then, without warning, the engine roared, and the car disappeared into the rain, leaving behind the unmistakable promise of what was to come.

Tory holstered her weapon, her expression grim. "If I'm going after Markham, I'll need help."

Antonio tilted his head. "You finally admitting you can't do it alone?"

Tory shot him a glare. "Don't get used to it."

"Wouldn't dream of it," Antonio said, his smirk widening.

Tory didn't smile. Her focus was already elsewhere, on the storm she could feel brewing.

The Veil's net was tightening, its threads invisible but inescapable. Hesitation wasn't an option—not when the storm was closing in. Whatever it took, whoever she had to face, Tory would be ready.

# CHAPTER 6
# MARKED FOR DEATH

THE RAIN HADN'T LET UP, TURNING the streets of San Francisco into a slick maze of shimmering reflections. The air was heavy with the metallic tang of wet pavement, and the hiss of tyres on rain-slicked roads echoed through the alleys. Tory Wayne's boots splashed through puddles, the cold seeping into her soles as she navigated the labyrinthine backstreets of the Mission District.

The Veil had officially put a price on her head.

It had started with whispers. Anonymous notes slipped under doors. Glances that lingered too long. Now, the threat was tangible, a bounty so large that mercenaries and syndicate enforcers alike had flooded the city looking for her.

Tory's hand rested on the pistol holstered under her jacket, her fingers brushing the cold metal for reassurance. The thought of being hunted gnawed at her, each shadow in the rain another potential threat. She wasn't afraid of a fight—she'd survived worse—but the bounty was different. It wasn't just the danger; it was the loss of control, the constant knowing that faceless predators were out there, hunting her for profit. Each step felt heavier, every shadow more hostile. It wasn't fear she felt—it was fury, a slow-burning anger at being reduced to prey.

———

SHE SLIPPED into an old laundromat on the corner, its buzzing neon sign barely holding on to life. The machines were silent, their drum doors open and waiting, but the space smelled faintly of detergent and mildew.

A figure was waiting at the back, hunched over a cracked laptop. Hank Waite looked up as she approached, his weathered face etched with concern.

"You look like hell," Hank said, motioning for her to sit.

"Feel like it too," Tory muttered, sliding into the chair across from him.

Hank, her former partner from her days as a cop, had been one of the few people she could still trust—mostly because he didn't ask too many questions.

"You're making waves," Hank said, tapping a few keys on the laptop. "Big ones. You know what they're saying out there?"

Tory leaned back, crossing her arms. "Enlighten me."

"Some people think you're working for The Veil. Others think you're trying to burn them down. Either way, you've made yourself a target."

"Good," Tory said flatly. "The Veil needs to know I'm not backing down."

Hank frowned. "You're playing a dangerous game, Wayne. You've got half the city chasing you, and the other half too scared to help."

Tory smirked faintly. "And yet here you are."

Hank sighed, rubbing a hand over his face. "Yeah, well, I've got a soft spot for lost causes."

———

HANK TURNED the laptop toward her, the screen displaying a series of encrypted files.

"These are from your USB drive," he said. "Took me all night to crack them, but I found something interesting."

Tory leaned forward, scanning the screen. Names and locations filled the list, but one stood out immediately: **Conrad Ellison.**

"The mayor," Tory muttered, her stomach twisting.

Hank nodded grimly. "Turns out, The Veil isn't just funding his campaigns. They've got him on a leash. Everything from zoning laws to police funding—it's all been tailored to serve their interests."

Tory's jaw clenched. "So Ellison's their puppet. What else?"

Hank hesitated. "There's an event coming up. A fundraiser at City Hall. Ellison's supposed to give a speech, but according to this—" He pointed to another file. "—it's a cover. The Veil's planning to use the event to finalize a deal with an international arms dealer."

Tory's blood ran cold. "If that deal goes through, they'll have enough firepower to turn the city into a war zone."

"Exactly," Hank said.

---

THE SOUND of a door creaking open sliced through the quiet, sharp and deliberate. Tory's pistol was in her hand in an instant, her body going still as her eyes swept the room. Footsteps followed, slow and measured, the kind that spoke of confidence. Hank cursed under his breath, his chair scraping back as he reached for his weapon.

Three figures stepped inside, their silhouettes framed by the neon glow from outside.

"Tory Wayne," one of them said, his voice calm but menacing. "The Veil sends its regards."

Hank cursed under his breath, reaching for his own weapon.

The first shot shattered the silence, ricocheting off a washing machine. Tory dove for cover, pulling Hank down with her as the gunfire erupted. The laundromat's windows exploded under the barrage, shards of glass scattering like icy shrapnel. The air filled with the acrid tang of gunpowder, the sharp cracks of gunfire reverberating off the tiled walls as the attackers advanced.

"They're not holding back," Hank muttered, firing a few shots toward the door.

"They never do," Tory replied, returning fire.

---

THE FIGHT WAS fast and brutal. Tory moved with precision, her training kicking in as she darted between cover, taking out one of the attackers with a clean shot to the chest. Hank managed to wing another, sending him crashing into a row of dryers.

The last man bolted for the exit, his footsteps pounding against the wet tiles. Tory was faster, the adrenaline driving her forward as she pursued him into the alley. She grabbed the back of his jacket, spinning him around before slamming him into the brick wall. The impact sent a crack through the night, and the man groaned, blood trickling from his mouth as he grinned through broken teeth.

"Who sent you?" she demanded, pressing her pistol against his temple.

The man grinned through bloodied teeth. "You're already dead, Wayne. You just don't know it yet."

Tory's finger hovered over the trigger, but she forced herself to pull back. Killing him wouldn't give her the answers she needed. Instead, she knocked him out with the butt of her gun and stepped back into the laundromat.

---

HANK WAS SITTING on the floor, breathing heavily as he reloaded his weapon.

"Well, that was charming," Hank muttered, wincing as he reloaded his weapon. "You sure know how to liven up a laundromat."

Tory grabbed a duffel bag from under the table, stuffing the laptop and files inside. "We've got to move. If The Veil knows we're here, it's only a matter of time before they send reinforcements."

Hank nodded, pushing himself to his feet with a groan. "Where to?"

Tory hesitated. "City Hall," Tory said, her voice firm. "That fundraiser isn't just a deal—it's their show of power. If we can stop it, expose what they're doing, we can cut their legs out from under them. Cripple their operation before they can cement their hold on the city."

"And probably get ourselves killed in the process," Hank said.

Tory smirked faintly. "You said you had a soft spot for lost causes."

Hank shook his head, muttering under his breath. "You're going to be the death of me, Wayne."

―――――

As THEY SLIPPED OUT into the rain-soaked streets, Tory felt the weight of the bounty pressing down on her. The Veil had marked her for death, but she wasn't going down without a fight.

The fundraiser was days away, but the clock felt like it was already running out. Tory's mind raced with possibilities, each one fraught with risk. The Veil had marked her for death, and City Hall would be crawling with their enforcers. But if she could stop the deal, even for a moment, it might be enough to tip the scales. She wasn't ready to die— not yet. But if the fight led her there, she'd make damn sure The Veil felt every ounce of her defiance, every move she made to tear their empire apart.

# CHAPTER 7
# ALL OR NOTHING

CITY HALL GLITTERED like a jewel in the heart of San Francisco, its marble façade gleaming under the harsh glow of spotlights. Inside, the air buzzed with murmured conversations and clinking champagne glasses, the scent of polished wood and floral arrangements masking the tension simmering beneath the surface. The rain had stopped, leaving the streets slick and shimmering as black sedans lined up in front of the grand steps. Inside, the fundraiser was in full swing, the city's elite mingling over champagne and whispered deals.

Tory Wayne stood in the shadows of a service entrance, her dark clothes blending into the night. Her heart pounded as she adjusted the earpiece Hank had rigged to their makeshift comm system.

"You're sure about this?" Hank's voice crackled in her ear, edged with tension.

"Not even a little," Tory muttered, pulling a compact pistol from her holster. "But if we don't stop this deal, The Veil gets enough fire-power to own this city."

"Markham's somewhere on the second floor," Hank said. "The arms dealer too. You've got to move fast."

"Got it," Tory replied. She slipped inside, her movements silent as she navigated the service corridors.

---

THE INTERIOR of City Hall was a study in decadence. Chandeliers sparkled overhead, their light casting a golden glow on the polished floors and grand staircases. Tory stayed in the shadows, her eyes scanning the room for threats.

From her vantage point, she spotted Mayor Conrad Ellison at the center of the crowd, shaking hands and smiling for photographs. He looked every bit the polished politician, but Tory knew better. Ellison wasn't just a pawn—he was complicit, his position a shield for The Veil's operations.

Tory's focus shifted to the second floor, where Markham stood near the railing, his sharp suit blending seamlessly with the wealthy guests around him. Beside him was a man she didn't recognize—tall, broad-shouldered, and exuding menace. The arms dealer.

"Markham's in sight," Tory whispered.

"Copy that," Hank replied. "I'll keep an eye on the perimeter. Be careful, Wayne."

---

TORY MOVED TOWARD THE STAIRS, slipping past a pair of guards with practiced ease. She reached the second floor and ducked behind a column, her eyes fixed on Markham and the dealer.

Their conversation was quiet but tense, their body language revealing the stakes. A briefcase sat on the table between them, and though Tory couldn't see inside, she knew it was the linchpin of the deal.

She tapped her earpiece. "I've got eyes on the deal. Going in."

"Wait," Hank said sharply. "You sure you want to do this alone?"

"I don't have a choice," Tory said.

---

As SHE MOVED CLOSER, a voice stopped her cold.

"Tory Wayne. Always in the wrong place at the wrong time."

She turned, her pistol snapping up, and found herself face-to-face with Antonio Alvarez. He was impeccably dressed as always, but there was no smirk this time, only a grim intensity.

"What the hell are you doing here?" Tory hissed.

"Same as you," Antonio said, his voice low. "Trying to stop a disaster."

"You're working with them," Tory accused.

"I'm working against them," Antonio countered. "Markham's deal isn't sanctioned by The Broker. If this goes through, it destabilizes everything."

"And I'm supposed to believe you?"

"You don't have to," Antonio said, his gaze steady. "But if you go in guns blazing, you'll blow our chance to take Markham down clean."

Tory hesitated, her instincts warring with her mistrust. "What's your plan?"

Antonio glanced toward the balcony. "We let the deal happen, but I take the briefcase. Without it, Markham's leverage evaporates."

"And if you double-cross me?"

"Then shoot me," Antonio said simply.

---

THE TENSION BETWEEN THEM CRACKLED, her instincts warring with the distrust that had kept her alive this long. Antonio's calm, unwavering gaze made it worse—like he knew she'd lower her weapon before she did. Finally, with a sharp exhale, she relented, the barrel of her pistol dropping a fraction. "Fine," she said, her voice tight. "But screw this up, and I won't hesitate."

"Fine," she said. "But if you screw this up, I'll kill you myself."

Antonio nodded, a faint flicker of amusement in his eyes. "Duly noted."

---

TOGETHER, they moved toward the balcony, staying hidden until they were just feet away from Markham and the dealer. The men were deep in conversation, their attention focused on the briefcase.

Antonio glanced at Tory, then stepped forward.

"Gentlemen," he said smoothly. "Hope I'm not interrupting."

Markham's head snapped up, his expression hardening. "Alvarez. What the hell are you doing here?"

"Keeping things orderly," Antonio said, his tone light. "You know how The Broker feels about unsanctioned deals."

The dealer frowned, his hand moving toward the briefcase.

Tory stepped out of the shadows, her pistol aimed squarely at Markham. "Nobody move."

The room erupted into chaos.

---

Markham lunged for his weapon, but Tory's shot caught him in the shoulder, sending him sprawling. The dealer grabbed the briefcase and bolted for the stairs, but Antonio was faster, tackling him to the ground.

Tory ducked as a guard fired at her, returning fire and dropping him with a clean shot. The sound of gunfire sent the fundraiser into a frenzy, guests screaming as they stampeded for the exits.

Antonio wrestled the briefcase free, but the dealer recovered quickly, landing a brutal punch that sent him staggering. Tory fired a warning shot, freezing the dealer in his tracks.

"Don't even think about it," she said coldly.

---

Markham, clutching his wounded shoulder, sneered at her. "You think this changes anything? You're just a pawn in a game you don't understand."

Tory aimed her pistol at his head. "Then explain it to me."

Markham's smirk widened, even through the pain. "The Broker's been watching, Wayne. Longer than you think. Every move, every choice—it's all been part of the plan. And you? You're the piece that changes everything."

Tory's chest tightened, Markham's words striking a nerve she didn't want to admit existed. Every instinct screamed to dismiss it as manipulation, but the way he smirked through his pain told her it wasn't a bluff. She forced her voice steady, her pistol unwavering. "Where is he?"

Markham laughed bitterly. "Closer than you think."

Before Tory could press him further, Antonio grabbed her arm.

"We need to go," he said urgently.

Tory hesitated, then nodded. They left Markham bleeding on the floor as they disappeared into the chaos.

---

OUTSIDE, the sirens grew louder as police swarmed City Hall. Tory and Antonio slipped into the shadows, the briefcase clutched tightly in Antonio's hands.

"What's in it?" Tory asked.

Antonio opened the case, the dim light catching the edges of a sleek encrypted drive and a thick stack of documents. Tory leaned closer, her eyes scanning the top page—a list of names. One jumped out at her, circled in red ink: **Wayne**. Her breath hitched, but before she could speak, Antonio snapped the case shut. "Enough to bury The Veil," he said, his voice low. "Or enough to start a war."

Tory stared at the files, her mind racing. Markham's words echoed in her ears: *This is about you.*

"What did he mean?" she asked quietly.

Antonio's expression darkened. "We'll find out. But if Markham's right, The Broker's been watching you for a long time."

Tory's jaw tightened. The city's chaos was just a tremor compared to the storm brewing on the horizon. Tory's grip tightened on the briefcase as Markham's words echoed in her mind. The Broker wasn't just watching—he was pulling the strings. And if this battle was about her, then she'd fight it on her terms.

The End

# EXPOSED

## A SHORT THRILLER

# CHAPTER 1
# THE MASTERMIND

THE SAFE HOUSE was silent except for the soft hum of the laptop, its glow casting faint light across the cracked walls. Tory Wayne sat at the table, her elbows propped up, her eyes locked on the files before her. The weight of the revelations pressed down on her chest like a physical force.

Elliot Moore.

Her mentor. Her trusted confidant. The one person who had believed in her when the department didn't. Now, she possessed evidence: he was not merely affiliated with The Veil; he was The Veil itself.

She clicked through the files, her hand trembling. Surveillance footage. Wire transfers. Photographs of Elliot at clandestine meetings with known criminals, faces she recognized from the syndicate and beyond. It wasn't just the city he controlled; it was a web of power that extended far beyond anything she'd imagined.

Behind her, Hank Waite leaned against the wall, his arms crossed. The years had worn on her former partner, the graying stubble on his chin and the weariness in his eyes a testament to a career of close calls and compromises.

"You sure about this?" Hank asked, his voice low.

Tory didn't answer immediately. She leaned back, staring at the ceiling for a moment before rubbing her temples. "I thought I was prepared for anything, but this..." She shook her head. "It's him, Hank. Elliot."

Hank exhaled sharply, pushing off the wall. "Elliot Moore? As in *your* Elliot? The person who supported you when Internal Affairs was about to abandon you?"

"The same," Tory said, her voice tight.

---

HANK SAT OPPOSITE, picking up a printout. It showed a list of transactions, each tied to shell corporations Elliot had used to launder The Veil's profits. The sums were staggering, the trail meticulous but undeniable.

"He's not just involved," Hank muttered. "He's running the whole damn thing."

"He always was too smooth," Hank added, his voice tinged with bitterness. I used to think it was simply part of his charm - the guy everyone aspired to be. But now? I wonder if the signs were always there, but we chose not to acknowledge them.

Tory nodded, her jaw tight. "He's been running it for years, right under our noses. And I think... I think he's been watching me. Guiding me."

Hank frowned. "Guiding you? What are you talking about?"

She pulled up another file, her stomach twisting as she scrolled. It was a series of case reports from her early days as a cop, all tied to The Veil. A pattern emerged—her assignments, her investigations, even her so-called successes—were all aligned with The Veil's goals.

"He let me think I was making a difference," Tory said bitterly. "But every arrest, every so-called win, was just part of his design. He didn't just use me—he built me into his plan."

Hank's face darkened as he leaned back in his chair. "That's messed up, even for this city."

Tory pushed the laptop away, her hands balling into fists. "I trusted him. He's the reason I became a cop in the first place. And now I find out he's been using me."

HANK WATCHED HER FOR A MOMENT, his expression softening. "So what's the play?"

Tory met his gaze, her green eyes blazing. "We expose him. Everything. His network, his connections, his crimes. We drag him into the light and watch his empire crumble."

Hank rubbed the back of his neck, clearly uneasy. "You make it sound simple, but this guy's been playing chess while we've been fumbling with checkers. You think he doesn't have contingency plans?"

"I don't care," Tory snapped. "He needs to be stopped."

Hank hesitated, then sighed. "Fine. But you're going to need help. Real help."

Tory arched a brow. "You offering?"

"I must be out of my damn mind," Hank muttered, shaking his head.

THE PLAN STARTED to take shape as they combed through the files. Elliot's web of power was vast, but Tory noticed a pattern—regular meetings at exclusive venues, often under the guise of legitimate business. Next night, a high-end Financial District restaurant hosted one meeting.

"This might be our only chance," Tory said, tapping the screen. "We need to know what he's planning and how deep it goes. If we don't get ahead of this, we're done before we even start."

"And if he spots you?" Hank asked.

"I won't let him," Tory replied.

Hank didn't look convinced. "Tory, this guy knows you better than anyone. You think you can just sneak around without him noticing?"

"I have to try," she said.

THE NEXT NIGHT, the city glimmered with rain-slicked lights, the Financial District alive with the muted bustle of wealth and power. Tory sat in the driver's seat of a borrowed sedan, watching the entrance to the restaurant from a block away.

Elliot arrived promptly at eight, stepping out of a sleek black car with the kind of poise that came naturally to someone who knew they were untouchable. Two men followed him inside—bodyguards, judging by their movements.

Tory's stomach churned as she watched him greet the host with his signature smile. It was the same smile that had disarmed her countless times, that had made her believe in justice when she wanted to walk away. She remembered the late nights in the precinct, his voice steadying her when the weight of the job felt unbearable. That man was a lie, and the realization burned in her chest like acid. For a moment, she felt like she was back on the force, a rookie looking up to the man who had taught her everything she thought she knew.

But that man didn't exist anymore.

---

SHE SLIPPED OUT of the car and moved toward the building, her hood pulled low. The service entrance was exactly where she'd expected, a discreet door near the rear alley. She picked the lock quickly, her movements precise, and slipped inside.

The kitchen was bustling, the heat and noise providing perfect cover as she made her way to the back stairwell. She climbed swiftly, her senses on high alert.

When she reached the second floor, she paused, listening.

Voices.

She edged closer, peering around the corner. Elliot stood near a large desk, his body language calm and controlled as he spoke on the phone.

"Everything's in motion," he said. "By tomorrow night, we'll lock down the tech sector. No complications, no mistakes. And make sure the contingencies are ready—just in case."

Tory's pulse quickened. She didn't know exactly what he was planning, but the pieces were falling into place.

---

As he ended the call, Elliot turned slightly, his eyes scanning the room. Tory froze, her breath catching. For a moment, it felt like his gaze lingered on her hiding spot, but then he moved toward the window, oblivious.

She slipped back the way she came, her heart pounding.

Back in her car, Tory gripped the steering wheel tightly. Elliot Moore was always two steps ahead. But this time, she wasn't going to let him win. The memories of his mentorship and betrayal churned in her mind, each one a bitter reminder of how far he'd shaped her life without her consent. She gripped the steering wheel, her jaw tightening. He wasn't untouchable—not anymore. For every lie he'd told her, for every time he'd used her, she was going to bring his empire crashing down, brick by brick.

He thought he was untouchable.

But she was going to prove him wrong.

# CHAPTER 2
# GATHERING FORCES

THE OLD WAREHOUSE on the city's edge was more fortress than refuge. Its towering walls of corrugated metal loomed over the fog-covered docks, and the faint hum of machinery from neighboring factories filled the air. Tory Wayne parked her sedan near the entrance, her gaze sweeping the area for anything out of place.

She was here to gather allies, but the truth was, she didn't trust any of them.

Hank Waite stepped out of the shadows as she approached, his hands shoved deep into the pockets of his weathered jacket. "You're late."

"I had to make sure I wasn't followed," Tory replied, her voice clipped.

Hank smirked faintly. "And were you?"

Tory didn't answer, pushing past him into the warehouse. The interior was dimly lit, the faint glow of overhead bulbs casting long shadows across stacks of abandoned crates. A small group of people waited near the center, their faces a mix of wariness and defiance.

Antonio Alvarez leaned casually against a crate, his sharp eyes tracking her every movement. His presence wasn't surprising, but it still set her teeth on edge. Tory remembered the first time she'd crossed paths with Antonio—years ago, during a sting operation that had gone sideways. He'd claimed to be working his own angles, but she had seen something then: a flash of anger when one of The Veil's men had casually referenced "collateral damage." Antonio wasn't just a cynic; he had his reasons for wanting The Veil dismantled. But he'd never shared what they were, and she wasn't about to ask.

"Always a dramatic entrance," Antonio drawled, his tone dripping with mock amusement.

"Not today," Tory shot back, her eyes sharp. "We've got bigger problems than your ego."

***

THE OTHERS WATCHED HER CLOSELY: a former cop named Mason, who'd been forced out of the department for refusing to play by the rules; Ellie Tran, a tech wizard who specialized in cracking encrypted systems; and Carla Vasquez, an ex-syndicate enforcer with a reputation for brutality. Each had their reasons for standing against The Veil, but trust was in short supply. Tory studied the group, their wariness palpable. Mason's jaw was tight, his hands twitching as if resisting the urge to bolt. Ellie avoided eye contact, her fingers fidgeting with the edge of her jacket, while Carla's sharp eyes moved from face to face, assessing weaknesses. It wasn't a team yet—just a collection of people bound by desperation and shared enemies.

"We're all here," Hank said, breaking the tense silence. "So what's the plan?"

Tory stepped forward, pulling a map from her bag and spreading it across a nearby crate. "Elliot Moore is The Broker. He's been running The Veil for years, using us—using the whole city—to consolidate power. If we're going to take him down, we need to hit him where it hurts."

She pointed to three locations on the map.

"These are critical to The Veil's operations: their financial hub in the Financial District, a communications relay in Chinatown, and a logistics center near the docks. If we can cripple these, we cut off their money, their coordination, and their supply chain."

Ellie frowned. "You're talking about a full-scale assault. How do you expect us to pull that off?"

"With precision," Tory said. "We'll split into teams. Each of you will have a target, and we'll move simultaneously. They won't know what hit them."

Carla leaned back against a crate, her voice laced with challenge. "So, while we're out making a mess, what's The Broker doing? Watching us on some high-tech feed and laughing his ass off?"

Tory's jaw tightened. "He's my target."

---

ANTONIO LET OUT A LOW WHISTLE. "You really think you can take him on alone?"

"I don't have a choice," Tory said, her voice hard. "This ends with him. If we don't cut off the head, The Veil will recover, no matter how much damage we do."

Mason nodded slowly, his face grim. "She's right. We need to take the fight to the top. But this kind of operation... people aren't walking away from it."

The room grew heavy with the weight of his words.

"I'm not asking anyone to risk their lives for me," Tory said, her voice steady. "But if we don't do this, The Veil wins. They take the city, and we'll never get it back."

Hank sighed, stepping forward. "We're with you, Wayne. Just tell us what you need."

---

THE REST of the group nodded, though their expressions varied from determination to reluctant acceptance. Tory handed out assignments, outlining the details of each team's mission. Ellie and Mason would handle the financial hub, using Ellie's tech skills to access and drain The Veil's accounts. Carla and Hank would take the logistics center, disrupting shipments and destroying supplies.

"And you?" Hank asked, his brow furrowed.

"I'm going after their communications relay," Tory said. "It's the key to coordinating their response. If I can take it offline, it'll buy us time to finish the job."

Antonio raised a brow. "No backup?"

"I work better alone," Tory replied.

---

As the meeting broke up, Antonio lingered behind while the others prepared to leave. Tory ignored him, focusing on folding the map and packing her gear.

"You're going to get yourself killed," Antonio said finally, his voice low.

Tory glanced at him, her expression hard. "You think I don't know that?"

Antonio stepped closer, his gaze intense. "Elliot's not just some syndicate thug. He knows you. He's been one step ahead this whole time. What makes you think this is going to be different?"

Tory's jaw clenched. "Because now I know who he is. And I'm not playing his game anymore."

Antonio smirked faintly. "You're stubborn. I'll give you that."

"Are you in or out, Alvarez?" Tory asked, her tone sharp.

Antonio hesitated, then nodded. "I'm in. But don't say I didn't warn you."

For a moment, Antonio didn't move, his gaze locked on Tory like he was searching for something—doubt, fear, hesitation. When he finally nodded, it was almost grudging. "You're too damn stubborn to let this go, aren't you?" he muttered. Then, softer: "Just don't make me regret this."

---

Later that night, Tory lingered outside the warehouse, the biting cold a welcome distraction from the weight of what lay ahead.

She thought of Elliot, his face a mask of calm power. He had played her for years, manipulated her every move.

This time, the game was hers to play.

Tory pulled her hood up and disappeared into the shadows.

# CHAPTER 3
# THE LAST ALLIANCE

THE CHINATOWN relay station blended seamlessly into its surroundings—a nondescript, two-story building wedged between a noodle shop and a fish market. The air was thick with the pungent mix of spices and damp concrete, masking the tension crackling in the cool night air. Tory Wayne crouched behind a stack of crates in the alley, every muscle taut as she scanned for movement.

Her comm crackled to life in her ear. Tory adjusted the earpiece, her pulse quickening. The weight of what they were about to do bore down on her, each decision sharpening into a blade. She knew this operation was their best shot at crippling The Veil, but the nagging voice in the back of her mind wouldn't let her forget how easily things could go wrong.

"Wayne, are you in position?" Hank Waite's voice was tense, the faint sound of machinery in the background betraying his own operation at the docks.

"Almost," Tory whispered. She adjusted the pistol at her side, her green eyes scanning the street for patrols. "What's your status?"

"Carla's planting the charges now," Hank replied. "Logistics hub will be toast in ten."

"Ellie and I are inside the financial center," Mason added over the comm. "Lots of resistance, but we're making progress."

Mason's voice was steady, but Tory could hear the strain beneath it —the sound of adrenaline and barely concealed doubt. A burst of static cut through the line, followed by Ellie's voice, quick and sharp. "Progress is generous. We've got more guards than we expected. If we don't find the server room soon, we're toast."

Tory clenched her jaw, forcing her voice to stay calm. "Stick to the plan. Prioritise the server room. Everything else is secondary."

———

TORY SLIPPED into the building through a side door, her movements silent. The interior was dimly lit, the faint hum of servers filling the air. Rows of machines blinked with LEDs, their steady rhythm a stark contrast to the chaos brewing outside.

She moved deeper into the station, her steps careful and precise. Her target was the central hub, a reinforced room at the heart of the building where The Veil's communications were coordinated. If she could disable it, it would leave their entire operation vulnerable.

But as she approached the hub, a voice froze her in her tracks.

"You're predictable, Wayne."

Antonio Alvarez stepped out of the shadows, his usual smirk replaced by a hard, unreadable expression.

Tory's hand shot to her pistol. "What the hell are you doing here?"

"Relax. I'm on your side—for now."

Antonio raised his hands in a gesture of mock surrender, his tone casual but his eyes sharp. "Making sure you don't get yourself killed before we finish this. Believe it or not, we're on the same side—for the moment."

"For now?" Tory echoed, her voice laced with suspicion.

Antonio stepped closer, his movements slow and deliberate. "You're not the only one who wants The Veil gone. But Elliot's not going down without a fight. You know that better than anyone."

TORY KEPT her pistol trained on him, her mind racing. She didn't have time for this—not now. "If you're here to help, start talking. Otherwise, get out of my way."

Antonio sighed, his smirk fading. "Fine. Elliot's not at his estate. He's here. Upstairs."

Tory's stomach tightened. "You're lying."

"Am I?" Antonio asked, arching a brow. "Why do you think he's been one step ahead this whole time? He's been monitoring every move you make. This relay station isn't just about communications— it's his personal nerve center."

Tory hesitated, her mind spinning. If Antonio was right, this changed everything. The thought of Elliot being so close sent a chill down her spine. Memories of his mentorship flashed through her mind —his calm voice guiding her through chaos, his steady gaze when everyone else doubted her. How much of it had been real, and how much had been manipulation? She shook the thoughts away. It didn't matter anymore. Elliot wasn't her mentor. He was her target. Taking down the relay station would still cripple The Veil, but if Elliot was here...

"Why are you telling me this?" she demanded.

Antonio's gaze hardened. "Because I've made my choice. I'm with you, Wayne. But if we're going to end this, we need to do it together."

---

TORY DIDN'T TRUST HIM—SHE couldn't. But she also couldn't ignore the possibility that Elliot was within reach.

"Fine," she said, lowering her pistol slightly. "But if you screw me over—"

"You'll shoot me," Antonio finished, his smirk returning faintly. "I'm well aware."

Together, they moved toward the central hub. Tory's heart pounded as they climbed the stairs, the tension in the air thick enough to cut. Every creak of the floorboards, every distant hum of machinery set Tory's nerves on edge. The hallway felt impossibly long, its shadows shifting with every flicker of the overhead lights. She exchanged a glance with Antonio, his expression unreadable but his steps as careful as hers. Neither of them spoke, the weight of what lay ahead silencing even Antonio's usual quips.

When they reached the top, Antonio gestured for her to stop. He pointed to a door at the end of the hallway, its frame reinforced with steel.

"That's it," he said quietly.

---

TORY MOVED CAUTIOUSLY, her pistol raised. She tried the handle—it was locked, as she'd expected. She motioned for Antonio to cover her as she pulled a small device from her pocket and began to work on the lock.

Seconds felt like hours as the mechanism clicked and whirred. Finally, the lock gave way, and Tory pushed the door open.

The room inside was a stark contrast to the rest of the building. It was sleek and modern, filled with high-tech equipment and screens displaying live feeds from across the city. At the center of it all stood Elliot Moore.

He turned slowly as they entered, his face calm, his sharp eyes assessing.

"Tory," Elliot said, his voice low and measured. "Right on time. I expected nothing less."

---

TORY'S GRIP tightened on her pistol. "It's over, Elliot. Your empire ends tonight."

Elliot smiled faintly, as if she'd just told a joke. "You really think it's that simple? I've built something far bigger than you can imagine. Even if you take me down, The Veil will survive. It's inevitable."

Elliot stepped forward, his calm gaze locking onto hers. "You've always been determined, Tory. It's one of your better qualities. But determination without foresight? That's dangerous. Every step you've taken tonight, every choice—it's all been anticipated. You're not dismantling The Veil. You're playing the role I wrote for you."

"I'll take my chances," Tory said, her voice cold.

Elliot's gaze shifted to Antonio, his smile widening. "And you, Alvarez? Still chasing scraps? Or have you finally found a spine?"

Antonio's jaw tightened, but he didn't respond.

---

THE STANDOFF WAS BROKEN by the sudden blare of an alarm. Tory's heart jumped as the screens flickered, displaying security breaches across the building.

"Looks like your friends are busy," Elliot said calmly. "You're out of time, Tory."

Tory stepped forward, her pistol aimed at Elliot's chest. "Shut it down. All of it."

Elliot raised his hands, his expression still infuriatingly composed. "Go ahead. Pull the trigger. But if you do, you'll lose the chance to end this for good. I'm the only one who can dismantle The Veil without leaving the city in chaos."

Tory hesitated, the weight of his words pressing down on her. Her mind churned as she replayed every decision, every sacrifice she'd made to get here. Was he right? Had she been moving pieces on his board all along? A flicker of doubt crept in, twisting her resolve. But then she remembered the faces of those The Veil had crushed—the lives destroyed by Elliot's ambition. She couldn't let him win, no matter the cost.

"Don't listen to him," Antonio said sharply. "He's bluffing."

"Am I?" Elliot asked, his gaze steady.

---

THE TENSION in the room was suffocating. Tory's mind raced as she weighed her options. Elliot was right about one thing—his death wouldn't magically fix the city. But letting him live felt like a betrayal of everything she'd fought for.

Finally, she lowered her pistol.

"Shut it down," she said again, her voice steely.

Elliot's smile faltered slightly as he moved to the control panel. With a few keystrokes, the screens began to darken one by one.

Tory kept her pistol trained on him as Antonio moved to secure the room.

"We're not done," Tory said quietly.

Elliot glanced at her, his expression unreadable. "No, we're not."

# CHAPTER 4
# THE CONFRONTATION

THE NIGHT SKY was thick with clouds, casting the city in shades of black and gray. Faint beams of light from distant streetlamps barely pierced the gloom, leaving the docks cloaked in a heavy, oppressive darkness. The air smelled of salt and diesel, and a chill breeze whispered through the towering stacks of shipping containers and crates. It was a place that felt forgotten by time, perfectly suited for The Veil's operations—hidden, efficient, and untraceable. In the distance, the faint wail of sirens echoed, a chaotic symphony underscoring the unraveling of The Veil. Tory Wayne crouched behind a stack of steel crates outside the logistics center, her earpiece buzzing with chatter from her team.

"Charges are set," Carla Vasquez reported, her voice tight but steady. "I'll give you the signal when it's time to blow."

"Copy that," Hank Waite replied. "Ellie, you good?"

"Almost there," Ellie Tran said, her voice tinged with frustration. "These servers are harder to crack than I thought. Just keep them off my back a little longer."

Tory's grip tightened on her pistol as she scanned the loading dock. The Veil's enforcers moved in pairs, their dark clothing blending with the shadows. They didn't know yet, but the operation was already slipping out of their control.

"We're running out of time," Mason warned. "If they catch on, we're screwed."

"Then let's make sure they don't," Tory said, her voice low.

---

ANTONIO ALVAREZ WAS BESIDE HER, his expression sharp as he watched the enforcers patrol the area. His shoulder was still stiff from the earlier fight at the relay station, but he hadn't complained once.

"They're ramping up security," Antonio muttered. "Elliot must've tipped them off before we cut the comms."

"Doesn't matter," Tory said. "We're too deep to pull back now."

Antonio smirked faintly. "You've got a flair for the cinematic, you know that?"

Tory's glare was sharp enough to cut. "You call it flair; I call it survival. Keep up or stay out of my way.

"***

The mission had been going too smoothly, and Tory knew better than to trust that luck. As if on cue, her comm crackled with Ellie's panicked voice.

"They're onto me!" Ellie hissed. "I've got two—no, three guys coming this way. I can't—"

Ellie's voice cracked with panic, the sound of shuffling and hurried typing in the background. Tory's grip on her pistol tightened as her pulse quickened. She could picture Ellie, crouched behind a terminal, her fingers flying across the keyboard as shadows loomed closer.

"Ellie, listen to me," Tory said, her voice steady. "Find cover. Don't engage unless you have to. Carla and Hank are en route."

"Easy for you to say," Ellie shot back, her breath ragged. "I don't have a gun, Tory—I have a keyboard!"

"Stay calm," Hank interrupted. "We'll get to you."

Tory's heart pounded. Ellie was deep in the financial hub, and the team was spread thin.

"I'll go," Antonio said, standing.

"No," Tory snapped, grabbing his arm. "We stick to the plan. Carla and Hank are closer. They'll handle it."

Antonio met her gaze, his expression unreadable, before nodding reluctantly.

---

TORY TURNED her attention back to the loading dock. The enforcers were converging on the logistics center, moving with precision that made her stomach churn. The Veil's power didn't come from brute force alone—it was their ability to outthink and outmaneuver their enemies.

"We've got movement," Mason said. "Five minutes, tops, before they figure out something's wrong."

"Then we hit them now," Tory said.

---

CARLA'S VOICE cut through the comms. "Charges are live. Give the word, and this place goes up in smoke."

"Hold," Tory ordered. She glanced at Antonio. "We need to clear the area first. Too many civilians nearby."

Antonio frowned. "And if we wait too long?"

"Then we improvise," Tory said.

He let out a low chuckle. "You really like to keep things exciting."

---

TORY'S MOVEMENTS were swift and purposeful, her footsteps muffled against the concrete. The first pair of enforcers didn't stand a chance— her pistol spat two silenced shots in rapid succession, each one finding its mark with cold precision. The guards crumpled without a sound, their bodies collapsing into the shadows. Antonio followed, his movements fluid as he dispatched another guard with a blade.

The air was thick with tension, every sound amplified by the stillness around them. Tory's senses were on high alert, her mind racing as she calculated their next move.

"Ellie?" she whispered into her comm.

"I'm clear," Ellie replied, her voice shaky. "Got what we needed. Heading to the rendezvous now."

Tory let out a breath she didn't realize she'd been holding. "Good. Carla, you're up."

---

THE EXPLOSION ROCKED the logistics center, a fiery bloom lighting up the night sky. The ground trembled as a deafening roar ripped through the air, the explosion's fiery bloom illuminating the docks in an eerie orange glow. The shockwave shattered windows and sent plumes of smoke spiraling into the sky. Flames licked at the metal walls, turning the once-organized facility into a scene of chaos and ruin. Tory shielded her face as shards of debris rained down, her ears ringing from the blast's force. The force of it sent shockwaves through the area, shattering windows and throwing debris into the air.

Tory and Antonio moved quickly, using the chaos to slip further into the facility. The enforcers were disoriented, shouting orders and scrambling to contain the damage.

"We're running out of time," Antonio muttered as they reached the central warehouse.

"Then let's finish this," Tory said.

---

INSIDE, the warehouse was a maze of crates and machinery. At its center was a command post, where a group of Veil operatives was frantically trying to coordinate a response.

Tory raised her pistol, her aim steady. "Drop your weapons!"

As she barked the order, her voice cutting through the chaos, a flicker of doubt pierced her resolve. These weren't faceless enforcers—they were people, caught in the same tangled web Elliot had woven. But she couldn't afford to hesitate. If they chose to stand with The Veil, they had made their decision, and she would not flinch in the face of it.

The operatives froze, their hands slowly rising. Antonio moved to secure the area, but one of the operatives lunged for a hidden weapon.

Tory fired without hesitation, the shot echoing through the cavernous space.

"Anyone else feeling brave?" she asked coldly.

The remaining operatives shook their heads, fear etched into their faces.

---

As ANTONIO SEARCHED FOR INTEL, Tory's comm crackled again.

"We've got a problem," Hank said, his voice grim. "Reinforcements inbound. Looks like Elliot sent backup."

Tory's stomach sank. "How many?"

"Enough to make this ugly," Hank replied.

Tory turned to Antonio. "We need to move. Now."

---

THEY REGROUPED OUTSIDE, the team converging near the docks. The glow of the burning logistics center lit up the night, casting eerie shadows over their faces.

"We got what we came for," Ellie said, holding up a hard drive. "Everything on their logistics operations."

"Good," Tory said. "But this isn't over."

Antonio stepped closer, his gaze intense. "Elliot's not going to let this slide," Antonio said, his voice low and edged with urgency. "You've taken the fight to him now, and he doesn't lose quietly."

Antonio didn't say what was on his mind: that Elliot wasn't just a target to him. Taking Elliot down was personal, a chance to erase years of guilt that had gnawed at him. He'd spent so long living in the shadows of The Veil, it felt strange to stand against it. But watching Tory risk everything to finish the job had stirred something in him—a reminder of the person he used to be before the compromises, before the losses.

Tory held his gaze, her expression unyielding. "He can throw everything he has. I've faced worse." She hesitated for a fraction of a second before adding, "But thanks for the warning."

---

As the team dispersed into the night, Tory lingered, staring at the smoldering ruins of the logistics center. The Veil was crumbling, but the cost was mounting.

She thought of Elliot—his calm, calculating demeanor, his infuriating certainty. This was the beginning of the end, but she knew the hardest part was still to come. Every move she made felt like a piece in his larger game, her victories tainted by the lingering question of whether she was still following his script. But tonight had been different. She'd taken control, disrupted his carefully laid plans. The flames licking at the night sky weren't just a symbol of The Veil's crumbling power—they were proof that she could win. And yet, the nagging doubt remained: how many steps ahead was Elliot now?

"I'm coming for you, Elliot," she murmured under her breath. "And this time, you won't see it coming."

# CHAPTER 5
# SECRETS EXPOSED

THE BURNED ruins of the logistics hub still smoldered as dawn broke over the city. Tory Wayne sat on the hood of a battered sedan parked along a quiet stretch of the docks, her eyes scanning the hard drive Ellie had handed her the night before. The files were dense, layered with encryption, but the pieces were starting to fall into place.

Elliot Moore wasn't just orchestrating The Veil's operations—he was embedding himself deeper into the city's infrastructure than Tory had imagined. The scope of his reach was staggering. Elliot wasn't content with controlling the syndicate—he was weaving The Veil into the city's fabric, using politicians as puppets, manipulating city budgets, and even swaying media narratives. Every detail in the files pointed to a level of control that bordered on omnipotence. Tory's stomach churned as she realised how methodically he had built his empire while staying invisible. His power didn't stop at criminal enterprises; it extended into politics, commerce, and even law enforcement.

"Ellie," Tory called without looking up.

The tech wizard leaned against the car beside her, sipping from a thermos of coffee. "What's up?"

"Run a search for connections to my old precinct," Tory said, sliding the laptop toward her. Ellie raised an eyebrow, her fingers already flying across the keyboard. "You sure about this? If he's tied to the cops, it's not going to be a surface-level connection."

"That's the point," Tory said, her tone steely. "I need to know who's been helping him pull my strings."

Ellie frowned but started typing. "You think he's still tied to the cops?"

Tory didn't answer immediately. Her gut told her the answer was yes, but she needed proof.

---

THE RESULTS CAME FASTER than she expected. Ellie whistled softly. "You're not going to like this."

Tory leaned over the screen, her chest tightening as she read the names scrolling past. Detectives, captains, even a judge she'd once trusted. All tied to The Veil.

Tory's breath caught as a name surfaced on the screen: Captain William Rourke. The man who had shaped her career, who had given her orders she thought were just. Now, his name sat there, a glaring indictment.

Tory's fists clenched. "Rourke's been in Elliot's pocket this whole time."

"Who's Rourke?" Ellie asked.

"My commanding officer," Tory said tightly. "He's the one who sent me undercover in the first place. The one who set me up to fail."

The pieces clicked into place with brutal clarity. Elliot hadn't just used her to take down his enemies—he'd orchestrated her fall from within the department.

---

ELLIE HESITATED. "TORY... THERE'S MORE."

Tory's breath hitched as Ellie pulled up a series of surveillance reports. Each one documented her movements from years ago, detailing her undercover work and her time as a rookie cop.

"They've been watching me since the beginning," Tory muttered, her voice barely audible. The weight of the reports felt like an anchor around her chest. Every undercover mission, every transfer, even personal moments she'd thought private—all reduced to cold, clinical observations. She clenched her fists, the betrayal cutting deeper than she'd anticipated. Elliot hadn't just monitored her—he had studied her, dissecting her life to turn it into a weapon.

"Looks like it," Ellie said softly. "And it wasn't just about The Veil. These reports go way deeper—stuff about your family, your old cases, even your personal life."

Tory stared at the screen, her mind reeling. Elliot had built his empire on manipulation, and she'd been his perfect pawn.

---

ANTONIO'S ARRIVAL was almost silent, his footsteps blending with the soft sounds of the docks. His eyes scanned the screen, his jaw tightening as he took in the damning evidence. "So, that's how he's been staying one step ahead. What else is in there?"

"Rourke," Tory said, her voice cold. "He's been working for Elliot since day one." Antonio's jaw tightened at the mention of Rourke. He'd had his own run-ins with the captain during his days as a smuggler. Rourke had turned a blind eye to The Veil's operations while cracking down on anyone who refused to play ball. It wasn't just Tory who'd been betrayed by the system. Antonio had been forced to cut ties with people he cared about—business partners, friends—just to keep from ending up on Rourke's hit list.

Antonio frowned. "That explains how Elliot kept tabs on you so easily."

"And why my first case went sideways," Tory added. "It was a setup from the start."

Antonio leaned against the car, his jaw tight. "So, what's the plan?"

"We take Rourke down," Tory said. "He's the last piece of Elliot's network in the department. If we expose him, we expose everything."

Antonio arched a brow. "And Elliot?"

"He's next," Tory said, her voice sharp with determination.

THE PRECINCT HAD CHANGED LITTLE since Tory's last visit. The smell of stale coffee and paper filled the air as she walked through the familiar halls, her steps confident despite the weight of what she was about to do.

Rourke's office was at the end of the corridor, the door ajar. Tory didn't bother knocking.

Rourke looked up from his desk, surprise flashing across his face before it was replaced by annoyance.

"Wayne," he said, leaning back in his chair. "This is unexpected."

Tory didn't waste time. She threw the hard drive onto his desk, her green eyes blazing. "Care to explain this?"

Rourke glanced at the drive, feigning confusion. "I don't know what you're talking about."

"Cut the crap," Tory snapped. "I know you've been working for Elliot. I've got the files to prove it."

FOR A MOMENT, there was silence. Tory studied his face, searching for a flicker of regret or shame, but there was none. Rourke had always been a commanding presence, the kind of leader people followed instinctively. Now, she saw him for what he was—a man willing to sacrifice anything, or anyone, to stay on top.

Rourke's expression hardened, but he didn't deny it. "You don't know what you're getting into, Wayne. Elliot's not someone you can just take down."

"I don't care," Tory said, her voice cold. "He's going down, and so are you."

Rourke leaned forward, his tone low and menacing. "You think this will change anything? The Veil isn't just Elliot. It's bigger than all of us."

"Maybe," Tory said. "But it ends here."

Before Rourke could respond, the door swung open, and Antonio stepped inside, his pistol trained on the captain.

Rourke's eyes widened. "You brought backup?"

"Insurance," Antonio said coolly, his pistol unwavering. "You've already made bad choices, Rourke. Don't add another to the list."

---

TORY TURNED BACK TO ROURKE, her voice steady. "Here's how this works. You're going to call Elliot and set up a meeting. You're going to tell him everything's fine—that I'm still on the run, that you've got it under control."

"And why would I do that?" Rourke asked, his tone defiant.

"Because if you don't," Tory said, leaning closer, "I'll make sure everyone knows exactly how deep you're in. You'll lose everything—your badge, your pension, your freedom. Do you really want to go down with him?"

Rourke's eyes darted between Tory and Antonio, weighing his options. Beads of sweat gathered on his brow, and his fingers hovered nervously over the phone. "And if I do call him? What happens then?"

"Then you get a chance to survive this," Tory said, her voice unyielding. "But don't mistake this for mercy, Rourke. You've already betrayed me once. You don't get another chance."

---

OUTSIDE THE PRECINCT, Tory leaned against the car, the adrenaline still coursing through her veins. Antonio stood beside her, his expression thoughtful.

"You think he'll play ball?" Antonio asked.

"He doesn't have a choice," Tory said.

Antonio nodded, then hesitated. "And after? What happens when Elliot realizes you're coming for him?"

Tory's gaze hardened, her voice quiet but resolute. "Then he'll understand what it means to face someone who has nothing left to lose."

# CHAPTER 6
# THE FINAL BATTLE

THE CITY GLIMMERED in the distance, its lights muted under a heavy canopy of clouds. Tory Wayne adjusted her grip on her pistol, her gaze fixed on the sprawling estate before her. The estate loomed like a fortress, its high walls and towering gates a testament to Elliot's obsession with control. Spotlights swept the grounds methodically, their beams slicing through the mist. Every detail screamed untouchable, yet Tory's team had already breached the perimeter. The thought sent a small flicker of satisfaction through her—Elliot's kingdom wasn't as invulnerable as he believed. Elliot Moore's fortress stood like a monument to his power—glass, steel, and sharp edges rising from meticulously groomed grounds.

Antonio Alvarez crouched beside her, his breath visible in the cold night air, his tone lighter than the tension warranted. Antonio tightened the sling around his shoulder, the pain a dull reminder of how close this fight had come to ending him. But that wasn't what kept him up at night. He thought of all the people The Veil had ground into dust —innocent or not. His past was stained, but he told himself he could balance the scales. Helping Tory wasn't redemption, not really. But it was a start.

"This is it. The part where I ask if you're sure about this and you give me a fiery comeback."

Tory's lips twitched in the ghost of a smile. "You know me too well."

Hank Waite's voice crackled over her earpiece. "Carla and I are in position near the west perimeter. Ellie's working on the power grid. You've got ten minutes before the lights go out."

"Copy that," Tory replied. "Stay sharp."

Antonio tilted his head. "You sound confident."

"Because I have to be," Tory said, shifting her focus back to the estate. "Let's move."

———

THE PERIMETER WAS HEAVILY GUARDED, but the chaos caused by Tory's team earlier had thinned the ranks. She and Antonio slipped through the shadows, taking out a pair of sentries with practiced efficiency.

Inside, the estate was eerily quiet. The opulence of Elliot's world was on full display—marble floors, grand staircases, and priceless artwork lining the walls. The air inside was thick with silence, broken only by the faint hum of hidden machinery. Every step Tory took seemed to echo, a reminder of how alone they were in this opulent maze. Her eyes darted to the artwork—a Rembrandt here, a Klimt there. Each piece told a story of power and wealth stolen from others. The estate wasn't just a home; it was a shrine to Elliot's domination of the city. Tory couldn't help but feel the weight of it all, the stark contrast between this lavish sanctuary and the damage it had wrought on the city.

"Where's our guy?" Antonio whispered as they cleared another hallway.

"Top floor," Tory said. "He's always looking down on everyone."

Antonio smirked faintly. "Appropriate."

———

THE HUM of machinery grew louder as they climbed, a subtle warning that Ellie's tampering had triggered a cascade of failures. When the lights flickered, the sudden plunge into partial darkness was both a blessing and a curse. Shadows deepened, turning the corridors into a labyrinth of unknowns. Tory tightened her grip on her pistol, the weight of what lay ahead pressing heavier with each step.

"Showtime," Ellie said over the comm. "You've got about five minutes before the backup generators kick in."

"Plenty of time," Tory muttered.

They reached the top floor without incident, the hallways eerily empty. Tory's stomach churned—Elliot was too smart for this to be a mistake.

As they approached the double doors at the end of the corridor, Antonio grabbed her arm. "You sure about this? He's not just going to roll over."

"I don't need him to," Tory said. "I just need him to fall."

---

THE DOORS SWUNG open under Tory's push, revealing Elliot Moore standing by a wall of glass overlooking the city. The room radiated power. Floor-to-ceiling screens lined one wall, displaying maps, data feeds, and live surveillance from across the city. A sleek desk dominated the center, cluttered with neatly arranged files and a glass tumbler of amber liquid. The space was meticulous, yet there was a palpable undercurrent of menace, as though the room itself conspired to keep intruders at bay. He didn't turn as they entered, his posture calm, his hands clasped behind his back.

"Punctual as ever," Elliot said, his tone laced with condescension. "I was beginning to wonder if you'd forgotten where to find me."

"Save it," Tory snapped, raising her pistol. "It's over."

Elliot finally turned, his sharp features illuminated by the faint glow of the city below. His expression was one of mild amusement, as if this were a game and he was still winning.

"You really believe that, don't you?" he said. "That you can end this with a gun and a few stolen files?"

---

Tory STEPPED CLOSER, her aim steady. "I've already ended it. Your network is gone. Your people are either in custody or running scared. You're alone, Elliot."

Elliot chuckled softly, shaking his head. "Do you think all of this crumbles because you pulled a few strings? The Veil isn't built on bricks or wires—it's built on people. As long as they're willing to look the other way, it survives."

"Not if I expose you," Tory said.

Elliot arched a brow. "Expose me to whom? The city? The same city that willingly turned a blind eye to everything I've done because they benefited from it? No, Tory. The Veil exists because people *want* it to exist."

Tory's FINGER hovered over the trigger, her anger bubbling over. "You twisted everything I believed in—turned my life into a tool for your empire."

Tory's voice cracked slightly, anger bleeding into hurt. "I gave everything to the badge because I believed in it. Because I believed in *you*. And all the while, you were pulling strings, making me your puppet."

Elliot's smile faltered, his tone softening. "You didn't become who you are despite me, Tory. Every skill, every triumph—you owe them to me. I built you."

"You gave me hell," Tory said, her voice shaking.

"And yet here you are," Elliot countered. "The only person capable of standing in my way. You should be thanking me."

Antonio, silent until now, stepped forward, his pistol aimed at Elliot's chest. "Enough of this. Drop the act."

THE TENSION SNAPPED like a taut wire. Elliot moved faster than Tory expected, pulling a hidden weapon from beneath his jacket. The tension snapped in an instant. Elliot's hand moved with deadly precision, pulling a compact pistol from beneath his jacket as he dove to the side. Tory barely registered the glint of metal before the first shot shattered the stillness, the glass wall behind him exploding into shards. Shots rang out, shattering the glass wall behind him.

Tory dove for cover, returning fire as chaos erupted in the room. Elliot darted behind a steel column, his movements surprisingly agile for a man his age.

The words seemed rehearsed, his defiance deliberate, as though he was clinging to the last vestiges of the invulnerability that had defined him. But behind the bravado, Tory glimpsed something deeper—a flicker of desperation, the faintest tremor in his voice. For all his calculated moves, Elliot had always been afraid of one thing: losing control. And now, as his empire crumbled around him, it wasn't the loss of power that terrified him—it was the mirror she'd forced him to face, one reflecting his own fallibility. The idea that he could be broken, just like everyone he'd manipulated, seemed to eat at him like acid.

"Do you really think this changes anything?" Elliot shouted over the gunfire. "Even if you kill me, there will always be someone else!"

"Not today," Tory muttered, firing again.

---

ANTONIO FLANKED ELLIOT, forcing him out into the open. Tory's shot clipped his arm, sending him stumbling to the floor. As Antonio moved, his mind replayed the night he had made his decision to turn against The Veil. It wasn't just business; it was personal. He thought of his brother—gone, thanks to one of Elliot's "necessary sacrifices" during an arms deal years ago. The memory of standing over the hastily closed casket had been enough to steel his resolve. This wasn't just about survival for him. It was retribution. She moved quickly, pinning him down with a knee to his chest, her pistol pressed to his temple.

"It's over," she said, her voice cold.

Elliot stared up at her, his calm façade finally cracking. "You can't kill me, Tory. If you do, you'll become exactly what I always knew you were—a monster."

Tory's grip on the pistol tightened.

"Don't do it," Antonio said quietly. "He's not worth it."

---

FOR A MOMENT, the room was silent except for the sound of their ragged breaths. Tory's mind raced, every memory of Elliot's betrayal crashing down on her.

Finally, she lowered the gun.

"You're right," she said. "You're not worth it."

She reached for the comm device at her hip, pressing a button to activate the livestream Ellie had set up.

"Say hello to the city, Elliot," Tory said, her voice filled with grim satisfaction. "You're exposed."

The screens around the room lit up, hijacked by Ellie's livestream. One by one, the faces of corrupt politicians, bought judges, and syndicate heads flashed across the displays, their crimes listed in stark detail. Tory's voice filled the air, projected over the feed. "This is Elliot Moore—the man who built The Veil and sold out this city. This is the truth he's spent years hiding."

Elliot's composure fractured further with every passing second, his eyes darting between the screens as his empire crumbled in real time.

Elliot's eyes widened as the realization sank in. Everything—the files, the confessions, the faces of those he'd manipulated—was being broadcast live.

"No," he whispered, his voice shaking.

"Yes," Tory said.

---

MINUTES LATER, sirens wailed as law enforcement swarmed the estate. Tory stepped out into the cold night air, her body trembling from the adrenaline.

Antonio joined her, his expression a mix of relief and exhaustion. "You did it."

"We did it," Tory corrected.

As dawn crept over the horizon, its light illuminating the shattered glass and burning wreckage of Elliot's empire, Tory felt the weight settle across her chest like a final breath before release. The city was free, but freedom came with scars—ones she wasn't sure would ever fully heal.

# CHAPTER 7
# AFTERMATH AND REDEMPTION

THE SUN HUNG low over San Francisco, painting the city in hues of gold and crimson. The dawn felt heavier than usual, the air thick with the remnants of smoke and ash. Somewhere in the distance, the faint cry of a seagull broke through the silence, a fleeting reminder that life continued, indifferent to the upheaval below. Tory felt the contrast keenly—the city's resilience against her own weariness.

Tory Wayne stood at the edge of the ruined estate, the jagged remains of Elliot Moore's empire silhouetted against the sky. Smoke still rose from parts of the grounds, the last echoes of the night's chaos dissipating into the cool morning air.

The city was quieter than she'd ever known it to be. The Veil's collapse had sent shockwaves through every layer of society, its intricate web of power torn apart in a single night. The Veil's collapse reverberated like an earthquake, shattering not just the criminal underworld but the fragile illusions the city clung to. What had been torn apart in a single night would take years to untangle, if it ever truly could be. But as she stared at the skyline, Tory felt no triumph—only the heavy weight of everything she'd sacrificed to get here.

HANK WAITE APPROACHED, his steps slow and measured. His jacket was torn, his face bruised, but he carried the same resolute energy that had kept him by her side all these years.

"They're taking him away now," Hank said, nodding toward the cluster of police cars in the distance.Hank's tone carried a strange mix of relief and resignation, as though the victory was already dimmed by what they'd lost along the way. "You did good, Wayne. Better than most would've, in your place."

Tory turned to him, her green eyes shadowed. "Better? I did what I had to, Hank. That's not the same thing."

Hank hesitated, then placed a hand on her shoulder. "Maybe not. But it's enough."

Tory didn't have to ask who he meant. Elliot had been dragged out of the estate in handcuffs, his calm demeanor finally cracking as cameras swarmed him.

"Think it'll stick?" Tory asked, her voice hoarse.

Hank looked past the flashing lights of the police cars to Carla, who stood at the edge of the scene, her face a mask of hard-earned resolve. 'Carla's staying on this, you know. She's got a ledger full of names and a fire in her I've never seen before.' He turned back to Tory, his expression softening. "This fight doesn't end tonight. She's just getting started."

Tory followed his gaze, catching Carla slipping the notebook into her jacket. The woman was relentless, but her crusade felt heavier now, like she was taking the weight of the city's ghosts with her. Tory had no doubt she'd make a difference—but at what cost? Carla had found her fight, but Tory wondered if she'd ever find her peace."

"It'll stick," Hank said. "Ellie's files are airtight. There's no crawling out of this one."

Tory nodded but didn't reply.

---

ANTONIO ALVAREZ LEANED against a nearby car, his arm in a makeshift sling from the injury he'd sustained during the fight. He watched Tory closely, his expression unreadable.

"So," he said, breaking the silence with a lopsided grin that didn't reach his eyes. "You've knocked the crown off the king. What's your next move?"

Tory turned, her green eyes meeting his. "You make it sound like I won."

Antonio smirked faintly. "Didn't you?"

She shook her head. "Elliot's gone, but The Veil... it's not just him. It's everyone who looked the other way. Everyone who let it happen because it was easier than fighting back."

Antonio straightened, his gaze hardening. "You can't take responsibility for the whole damn city, Wayne. You did your part. That's more than most people can say."

Tory didn't respond.

---

THE SOUND of boots on gravel drew her attention. Ellie Tran approached, her laptop bag slung over one shoulder. The exhaustion in her face was unmistakable, but there was a glint of something fierce in her expression—a satisfaction hard-earned and deeply personal.

"It's done," Ellie said. "The livestream reached every major network. Everyone saw what Elliot was, what he did. They can't ignore it now." Her voice held a quiet triumph, but there was something deeper underneath—a weight that even victory couldn't lift completely. "This was never just about exposing him. It was about proving that someone—anyone—could stand up to him. To all of them. My brother didn't get that chance, but maybe now, someone else will."

"Good," Tory said, though her tone lacked conviction.

Ellie hesitated, glancing at Hank and Antonio. "What about you? You okay?"

For a moment, Ellie's professional demeanour slipped, and something raw flickered in her eyes. "You know, when The Veil came for my brother, I thought I'd never have the chance to fight back. He was just a name on a list to them, another loose end tied to their deals. That's what got me into this—making sure no one else loses someone like I did." She let out a shaky breath, her usual confidence edged with vulnerability. "So yeah, I'm okay. For the first time in a long time, I think we actually made a difference."

---

As the others drifted back toward the cars, Hank lingered.

"You sure you don't want a lift?" he asked.

Tory shook her head. "I need some time to think."

Hank gave her a long look, then nodded. "Take care of yourself, Wayne. And don't be a stranger."

As Hank walked back to the cluster of police cars, Tory watched him exchange a quiet word with Carla, who was leaning against the hood of a squad car. Carla's sharp edges seemed softened in the pale morning light as she handed over a battered notebook—a ledger from one of The Veil's safehouses.

"Evidence or insurance?" Hank asked, tucking it into his jacket.

"Both," Carla replied. Her voice carried a weight Tory hadn't heard before—a quiet determination to rebuild something out of the ashes.

Hank clapped her on the shoulder. "You sticking around?"

Carla shrugged. "Not much else to do. Might as well see if the city's worth fighting for without them pulling the strings."

Tory felt a flicker of something like hope as she turned back toward her car. The fight wasn't over for them either—but at least it was theirs now.

---

The city was waking up now, the distant hum of traffic picking up as people began their day. Tory stood there for a long time, her mind replaying the events of the past few months. The betrayals, the losses, the fleeting moments of hope—it all felt like a blur, too big to fully process.

She thought of the people she'd lost along the way, the ones who had believed in her even when she hadn't believed in herself. She thought of the young rookie she had been, standing in the precinct for the first time, eager to prove herself in a world that thrived on compromises. She remembered the sting of betrayal when her first case fell apart and the quiet moments when doubt nearly drowned her resolve. Each loss, each failure, had carved a piece of who she had become. It wasn't just Elliot who had shaped her; it was the sum of every choice, every sacrifice.

Elliot's parting words lingered like a stain: *You'll become exactly what I always knew you were—a monster.* But they no longer had the power to pierce her. She'd carried the weight of his manipulation long enough, and now she saw the truth. She wasn't a monster. She was the reckoning.

But Elliot had been wrong. The fire he'd tried to ignite within her hadn't consumed her—it had tempered her. She had walked through his gauntlet, not as a puppet or pawn, but as something more. She wasn't defined by his games or his schemes. The monster he tried to create had instead become a fighter, someone who stood against the darkness instead of succumbing to it.

———

By the time she returned to her car, the others were gone. She slid into the driver's seat, the leather cold against her skin.

A folded piece of paper sat on the dashboard, its edges slightly crumpled as if it had been clenched in a fist before being placed there. She opened it, her brow furrowing at the single line written in Antonio's sharp handwriting:

**Don't let the city keep you. You deserve better.**

Beneath the words, there was a faint, almost hesitant addition—barely legible but unmistakable:

Some of us never had that choice.

Tory crumpled the note in her hand, her jaw tightening. The weight of his words settled over her, heavier now with the subtle admission scrawled beneath. Antonio, for all his bravado, had lived his life in the city's grip—bound by its shadows and hardened by its betrayals. The note wasn't just a parting thought; it was a confession of regret, a warning, and maybe even a plea. Tory stared at the crumpled paper in her hand, a knot tightening in her chest. He was giving her something he'd never had—a chance to walk away.

---

As THE TIRES hummed against the wet pavement, Tory's hand brushed the edge of her jacket pocket. Inside, she felt the familiar shape of her father's old badge—something she hadn't looked at in years. It had been her compass once, a reminder of why she'd joined the force in the first place. She pulled it out, the tarnished metal catching the faint glow of passing streetlights.

The badge was battered, like her, but it still held weight. Her father used to say it wasn't just a symbol of law and order—it was a promise to protect people, even when it wasn't easy. Tory's grip tightened around it. She wasn't a cop anymore, and the city's scars weren't going to fade overnight. But maybe—just maybe—there was still a way to keep that promise.

She drove aimlessly for hours, the city blurring past her. Every turn brought her past another ghost. The diner where she and Hank had celebrated their first major bust. The precinct steps where Elliot had once told her she was destined for greatness. The street corner where she'd made her first arrest. Each landmark felt more like a gravestone, marking the death of the life she thought she'd wanted. The places she passed were no longer just streets and buildings—they were memories, pieces of a life she'd fought to reclaim but no longer recognized.

When she finally stopped, it was at the edge of the bay, the waves lapping against the rocks in steady rhythm. The water stretched out before her, vast and unknowable, reflecting the faint glow of the city behind her. She stepped out of the car and onto the shoreline, the cold wind biting her skin, and let the enormity of it all settle around her.

The wind bit at her cheeks, carrying the salty tang of the ocean and the distant creak of boats swaying in the tide. She stood there, letting the cold seep in, as though it might strip away the layers of pain and doubt. The horizon was painted in muted colours, a quiet promise of something beyond the city's boundaries.

Tory stepped out of the car, the wind whipping her hair as she stared out at the horizon.

Tory unclasped the badge from her palm, staring at it one last time before tucking it back into her pocket. She didn't need it to remind her anymore; the choices she'd made, the battles she'd fought—they'd shaped her as much as any badge or title ever could.

She thought about the people who had stood beside her—Hank, Ellie, Antonio. Each of them carried their own burdens, but they'd chosen to fight anyway. She smiled faintly at the thought. Maybe there was something worth saving, even in a place as broken as this city.

The city lay behind her, a broken battlefield scarred by the weight of secrets and shadows. Those scars had marked her too, etched into her soul like a map of every wound and triumph. They would never fade completely, but as she watched the morning light spill across the horizon, she realized they didn't have to. Those scars were proof of her survival, of her strength. They weren't just marks of what she'd endured—they were a map of every choice, every person she'd fought for, and every moment she'd found herself again. The scars weren't just reminders of what she'd lost; they were the reason she still stood, the reason she could still look forward and believe in something beyond the city's shadows. It wasn't about erasing the past—it was about carrying it with her, not as a burden, but as a foundation. And for the first time in years, she felt the faint stirrings of freedom—not as an escape, but as a choice.

With a final glance back at the skyline, Tory let the weight of the city's battles settle over her—loss for the lives taken, relief for what she'd reclaimed, and hope that the scars left behind might lead to something better. The map on the passenger seat caught her eye, its creases and folds a reflection of her own journey. It wasn't the city's streets she saw anymore—it was the open highways, each road a promise of choices she'd never had before. She reached for the engine, the hum of the car becoming a steady rhythm to match the stirring resolve inside her. Somewhere ahead lay something worth finding, and for the first time, it was hers to choose.

The End

Did you enjoy *City of Lies*?

Please consider reviewing it on Goodreads, Bookbub, or your favorite retailer. Reviews help me reach new readers.

**Please let me know if you want more stories featuring Tory Wayne.**

Join my newsletter for writing updates, sales, and promotions.

# ABOUT THE AUTHOR

Sam Chase delivers heart-pounding thrillers crafted for quick reads. Whether you're commuting, relaxing, or need a break, these stories will keep you on the edge of your seat.

**Website**: www.samchaseauthor.com

**Newsletter**: samchaseauthor.substack.com

𝕏 x.com/samchaseauthor

a amazon.com/author/samchasemystery

BB bookbub.com/authors/sam-chase-0987d23f-73d9-4b97-9954-5f9fce0c0ce3

g goodreads.com/samchaseauthor

# ALSO BY SAM CHASE